This was a moment that should be shared between lovers,

Lucia thought, drawing her knees up and looking out at the ocean. I'm in love with him again, she realized as the soft night air washed over her. No...she had never fallen out of love with him. But she had known from the beginning that Ryan had no desire for a lasting commitment. He had told her as much.

She smiled slightly, remembering how adamant she had been in return. She, too, had been wary of commitment and had seriously doubted that she would ever marry.

It had been easy to assure Ryan that she had no interest in a future together, but that assurance had slowly become a lie. Maybe not so slowly, she admitted now. It was as if from the moment they met she had known he was the right man for her. And no matter how much she tried to deny it to herself, things hadn't changed.

She'd loved him then, and she loved him now.

Dear Reader,

Merry Christmas! This is the season for good wishes and gift giving, and I hope that one of your gifts to yourself this holiday season will be the time to read this month's Silhouette Intimate Moments. As always, we've put together what we think is a pretty special package for you.

For starters, try Marilyn Pappano's *Room at the Inn*, a very special—and especially romantic—book set around a country inn, the holiday season and, of course, a man and a woman who are destined to be together forever. Snow is falling in tiny Angel's Peak, North Carolina, when Leah meets Bryce for the first time. How can she know that he's the man who will change her life and bring joy to her heart, becoming not only her husband but a father to the four children she loves so much? There's "room at the inn" for you, too, so why not join her for a very special Christmas?

Then, if you're tired of winter, escape into summer with ever popular author Heather Graham Pozzessere. *Lucia in Love* reignites Lucia Lorenzo's once torrid relationship with Ryan Dandridge. With her entire lovable, wacky family on hand, Lucia expects their reunion to be eventful, but never downright dangerous! And Ryan isn't the only threat; someone else is stalking her. Surrendering to Ryan might very well be the *best* thing she could do.

Complete this month's reading with new books from Mary Anne Wilson and Doreen Roberts, then look forward to next year and more compelling romances from your favorite authors, including Maura Seger, Linda Howard and Barbara Faith, to name only a few.

Happy Holidays!

Leslie J. Wainger
Senior Editor

Heather Graham Pozzessere
Lucia in Love

Silhouette Intimate Moments

Published by Silhouette Books New York

America's Publisher of Contemporary Romance

SILHOUETTE BOOKS
300 East 42nd St., New York, N.Y. 10017

ISBN: 0-373-07265-1

First Silhouette Books printing December 1988

Printed in the U.S.A.

Books by Heather Graham Pozzessere

Silhouette Intimate Moments

Night Moves #118
The di Medici Bride #132
Double Entendre #145
The Game of Love #165
A Matter of Circumstance #174
Bride of the Tiger #192
All in the Family #205
King of the Castle #220
Strangers in Paradise #225
Angel of Mercy #248
This Rough Magic #260
Lucia in Love #265

HEATHER GRAHAM POZZESSERE

considers herself lucky to live in Florida, where she can indulge her love of water sports, like swimming and boating, year-round. Her background includes stints as a model, actress and a bartender. She was once actually tied to the railroad tracks to garner publicity for the dinner theater where she was acting. Now she's a full-time wife, mother of four and, of course, a writer of historical and contemporary romances.

Dedicated with love to my own Italian in-laws:

The Pozzesseres...

The Antinerellas; Auntie Chris and Genie; Auntie Virginia; the Ostrouts (all of them); Angie and Al (Nana and Papa Pozzessere); the Crosbies, Auntie Alice and Uncle Buppie, Ginger, Linda, Mary and all; Auntie Tina, with lots of love; Helen, Mary Anne, and Frankie Pozzessere and the kids in Worcester; Auntie May and the Dursos; Uncle Willie and Auntie Peggy and Debbie, Donna, and Diane. In memory of Tony and Armand. To all of the cousins and second cousins, and very especially, Jimmy and Gail—I cannot imagine life without you both, you are so very special.

The Meros...

Uncle Frank and Auntie Grace upstairs (Astrella), Auntie Grace and Uncle Frank downstairs (Mero). Uncle Johnny and Auntie Joan Mero, Uncle Sal and Auntie Ida Mangiulli. To Auntie Dee and Uncle George Law, who adopted all six of us so lovingly.

And to the cousins and their families, all of them, Joyce and Janet, Davey and Francis, Raymond and Paul, and to Bobby and Helen and the baby, Eileen and Eddie and Dennis and David, to Kenny and Doreen, and to Kim, and Brent, and very especially Donna and Richard Astrella, because I know that Richard will keep a copy at the Orange Savings Bank.

And to my own little Pozzesseres, with all my heart;

Jason, Shayne, Derek and Bryee-Annon,
And to their father, Dennis, with all my love.

Thank you all for the laughter and the love.
Nobody does it better!

Chapter 1

It wasn't that she hadn't been expected to encounter another person in the bed because she had.

She had known someone else was there when she had crawled in last night—or early that morning, actually—about two o'clock. She had been supposed to share the room with someone, anyway, so the fact that something had changed and now she was also sharing the bed didn't seem too odd.

This simply wasn't the right someone.

She discovered that fact slowly. She could only explain the time it took her to discover what should have been an obvious mistake by reminding herself that she was absolutely exhausted; she had worked a full day and half the night, then driven in circles for hours, and she was still so tired that she simply didn't want to wake up.

The legs should have been her first—and most important—clue. Beyond a doubt, those legs did not belong to her cousin Dina, and Dina was the someone who should have been sharing the bed. Dina's legs were long and slim. These legs were long, but they were also hard and heavily muscled, covered with coarse hair—and indisputably masculine.

But Lucia had been so exhausted that it hadn't registered that the legs were all wrong. On the contrary, they had seemed to be just right.

Perhaps that was the real problem.

Some warning should have sounded, even in her exhausted state. Some instinct should have told her that this wasn't right at all.

The body beside her was long, and it was warm. She had begun the night on the edge of the bed—just as the other body had. When they were kids, she and Dina had shared a double bed dozens of times—with half their other female cousins thrown in for good measure. They had often slept up in Grandma's big bed, where they had poured out their dreams and their fantasies. But those days were long ago now; she and Dina were supposed to share a room in the condo, but not a bed.

Still, when Lucia had arrived and found only the one bed, she had assumed that Aunt Faith had flubbed things a bit. There were twenty-six family members here: the Three Graces, as she and her cousins referred to her aunts—Faith, Hope and Charity—their husbands, and various children and grandchildren. Patience, Lucia's mother, had been unable to make it to the reunion because her husband had taken her on an anniversary trip. Lucia's mother was aptly named, the cousins had all decided. Patient and soft-spoken, she was younger than the Three Graces, and the cousins had agreed the calmest of the group.

Now, fully awake, Lucia pulled her mind back from thoughts of her family and realized that something had gone wrong. At 2:00 a.m. it had been very easy to assume that Aunt Faith had assigned her and Dina to the wrong room, and that the figure asleep in the bed was Dina.

But as morning dawned and she felt those hairy legs, Lucia began to realize that the body next to her did not belong to Dina. And yet she felt an instinctive sense that things that should have been entirely wrong were entirely right....

She had begun the night on the edge of the bed, but as the hours passed she had moved toward the center of the bed. But she had been sure that what followed was a dream.

In the dream, she had curled into the middle of the bed with Ryan, as she so often had. He had slipped his arm around her and held her close. It was the way they had always slept. His chin would rest on the top of her head, his fingers would lie idle over her abdomen and she would feel completely secure and feminine. She would feel the radiating warmth of his naked flesh, and smile, knowing that a matching smile would be curving his lips, because he would be awakening. His fingers would begin slowly stroking over her belly, then wander to her breasts. No matter how soundly she slept, the seduction of his touch would always call to her. It would reach into her dreams, rush through her blood, haunt her flesh, and before she had even fully awakened, she would be turning to him, want-

ing him. Often she would open her eyes wide with
surprise and meet his, blue-green eyes, sea eyes, full of
mischief, darkening with passion. Then she would feel
the tension in his body and the pressure of his lips, and
the sweet hunger would burst upon her, and she would
be very, very much awake. . . .

That was what *had* been, Lucia reminded herself.
Past tense. Ryan was no longer part of her life.

Yet she felt as if she might have been back with him.
Still in a state somewhere between sleep and waking,
she thought back to those days in December when he
had entered into her life and her world had suddenly
begun to revolve around him completely, when he had
begun to mean everything to her. Back to the night
when they had argued so horribly, when she had realized that he was only a comet shooting across the
sky, a comet that she could never catch and certainly
never hold.

The body next to her shifted, and once again she felt
the touch of those masculine legs.

Lucia stiffened, and full awareness rushed through
her. She wasn't dreaming. She *was* lying there, curled
up beside someone with long, masculine legs and long,
bronzed fingers that lay beneath her breasts and an
arm that curled nonchalantly over her waist. His
hands were powerful looking, his nails were bluntly
clipped and clean, and he wore a sport watch with a
black band.

She screamed, not a cry of terror, but rather one of
shock and abject dismay and absolute disbelief.

She reached for the fingers beneath her breast, but
her cry had startled him awake, and that long-fingered
hand was suddenly clamped over her mouth. She

twisted around and came face-to-face with Ryan Dandridge.

In those first few seconds Lucia was certain that he was just as startled as she was. His tawny brows shot up, and then his sea-colored eyes narrowed sharply on her, and it seemed as if a mask of suspicion fell over his features.

It was his angry look. She knew it all too well. It was dark and ominous and implacable. If he had been standing, he would have locked his arms over his chest. But he wasn't standing. He was lying down, with his hand still clamped over her mouth and his leg cast over hers. His bare leg. His chest was bare, too, she saw. Bare and bronze and covered with coarse tawny hair. She wondered what else was bare. She burned inside at just the thought and was afraid that she had also turned crimson at it.

It didn't matter, because he couldn't be here. She was in Garden City, South Carolina, and she hadn't seen him in months—not since she had left him in Rhode Island. He was supposed to be her cousin Dina Donatello. But he *was* here, and he was clearly furious.

"What the hell are you doing here?" he exploded.

Trust him to have the arrogance to ask such a stupid question when he was so clearly in the wrong—not to mention preventing her from giving him an answer!

She twisted frantically, and his hand fell from her face. Before she knew it, she was shouting at him with a vengeance. "What am *I* doing here? Get out of this bed! Get out of this room before I call the police. How did you find me? What the hell did you think you could possibly accomplish by coming here? Where's Dina? What have you done with her? You—"

He grabbed her chin and interrupted her. "Shut the hell up, Lucia, will you, please? I imagine people are still trying to sleep nearby."

She jerked against him violently, freeing herself from his not-at-all tender grasp. "Get off of me!"

She stared at him, hating him, in a way. She had convinced herself of that—it had seemed to be the only way to live without him at the time. But suddenly, seeing his tousled hair, his striking eyes and blunt, powerful features, she thought of the first night she had seen him. She had been eating lobster with a client while a band played and couples whirled around the dance floor. She had looked up and seen him; he had been watching her. He hadn't looked away. He had smiled, and she had blushed and stumbled over the simple explanation she was giving her client about the properties of golden oak, and then she had discovered herself looking up again.

He had still been staring at her.

Then someone tapped him on the shoulder, apparently a colleague, but he had shaken his head and smiled, and Lucia had felt her breath quicken as she had watched him walk straight toward her. He had excused himself pleasantly to Jim Dyson, her client, and then he had reached for her hand and pulled her straight out to the dance floor.

He had been tall and handsome and determined, and his smile had been incredibly charming. On the dance floor she had pulled herself up to her full five foot three and, with great dignity, informed him that she was with a client, that she didn't dance with strangers, and she intended to return to her booth.

"What's your name?" he had asked her.

"Lucia. Lucia Lorenzo."

"Lucia." He ran her name over his tongue, as if he were tasting it and finding it sweet. Then he had pulled her closer and told her that his name was Ryan Dandridge, and that they weren't strangers anymore. It was true. In those seconds it seemed as if she had somehow come to know him very well. To know the feel of his arms, and the special magnetism of his scent and the compelling attraction of his eyes, of his smile. To know his warmth, and the curious security she felt in his embrace as they danced.

He walked her back to her table, thanked Jim and said casually that he would see her later.

"Friend of yours?" Jim had asked.

And, inexplicably, she had answered yes.

That had been the beginning....

Now he suddenly released her. He stared at his hands as if he had touched fire, then looked back to her sharply. "What are you doing here? What the hell are you doing here?"

"Me?" she asked. His leg was still on top of hers, and the Snoopy nightshirt she had quickly struggled into last night was bunched high on her thighs, letting his bare flesh touch hers. He seemed even more muscular than she had remembered, and she realized that he probably *was* entirely naked; she just didn't have the nerve to look.

She lifted her eyes to meet his. She expected to meet a sardonic smile, but he was still staring at her angrily, though. There was also something slightly puzzled about the look on his handsome features.

"Well, Ms. Lorenzo, what are you doing in my bed?"

"You're in *my* bed!" she shrieked.

"I beg to differ." His eyes slid over her, and the sardonic smile she had expected earlier fell into place. "Not that I mind having you here."

"Bastard!" she hissed, and before she knew what she was doing she seized a pillow and bashed it against his head. He hadn't been expecting the attack, and it slammed him down flat on the bed.

She heard him swear and prepared for a fast flight. She had almost cleared the bed when his fingers clamped around her arm and he pulled her toward him. Her nightshirt bunched up all the way, and she gasped, startled, when he straddled her waist. Beyond a doubt, he was naked. Naked and very male.

The fabric of her nightshirt barely covered her breasts. She was wearing only a pair of lace bikini panties beneath the nightshirt, and those seemed to cover nothing. She felt him as strongly as she might feel the heat of the sun. She swallowed, fighting to remain calm, to maintain some kind of control. He seemed completely at ease, unmindful of their state of undress. He didn't even seem to care that it was obvious that she still had an effect on him.

"Stop this!" she said, but it was a whisper and not a demand.

"Isn't this why you're here?" he asked quietly.

"What?" She had to be losing her mind.

He smiled, but it was a dry smile, bitter. "This *isn't* why you're here? Then why? You left in the middle of a discussion, as I recall. Are we picking it up again now? You just came to talk? Really? So why crawl into my bed?" His gaze swept over her again. "I should warn you, though, that if you really intended to seduce me, something in black lace might have been a little better. Snoopy is cute, but . . ."

She let out an inarticulate oath and attempted to dislodge him. It was impossible. Her temper rose, and so did her panic. She couldn't stand to be near him. It was too painful. It had been too hard to learn to live without him. This wasn't a dream, it was a nightmare. A nightmare come true.

"Move!" she commanded him.

"Oh, I get it. You crawled in here just to get into another argument. Forget it, Lucia. You left me once. I don't want any explanations—"

"And I'm not going to give you any!"

"You shouldn't have come. I might have had another woman in my bed. What would you have done then?"

"You are the most insolent man I have ever met in my entire life! I am *not* in your bed!"

"Lucia!" His lip curled, and then he laughed. His thighs tightened around her, and she felt the explosive heat of his body and the rigid strength of him. "One more for old times' sake, is that it?"

"No!" This was impossible. She hated the way he was looking at her, and yet he felt so good. She had completely lost her mind!

She had to get away from him. She was suddenly afraid that she was going to cry.

Tears welled in her eyes, and she blinked them back furiously, dismayed at the emotion that seized her. She had done the right thing when she left him. Their argument had been bitter and awful, and nothing good could have come from it. They simply weren't meant to be together. ·

But she hadn't done well without him. Sleeping alone, waking alone. Dreaming. God, she had missed him. The feel of him, the scent of him. His whisper, his touch.

"Please! Ryan, please move. Let me up!"

Her words tumbled out desperately. Some of her emotion spilled into her voice, and he released her instantly, but he still hovered over her, his eyes guarded, his mouth set. His cheekbones were high and square, and his expression could be ruthless. Though a lock of his hair tumbled over his forehead and he was vulnerably bare, there was nothing unguarded about him.

"Ryan, please!"

He moved away from her, and she took immediate advantage of her freedom. She leaped to her feet and walked over to the door, then turned around, bracing herself against it. He had drawn up the sheets and sat Indian-style, with the covers stretched across his knees. His hands were folded in his lap, and he was still staring at her, accusing her.

"What are you doing here?" he asked again.

"What are *you* doing here?" she repeated desperately.

"I own this place."

"What?"

"I own it." He waved a hand, indicating their surroundings. "I built this place, Ms. Lorenzo. This is what I do for a living, remember? The time I devoted to my career was a bone of contention between us. Or so I thought. Maybe that wasn't it at all.''

She ignored the bitter taunt. "You . . . own this?"

"Yes."

Lucia swallowed.

He arched a brow, and his sardonic smile curled into place. "You didn't know that? Come on, Lucia. So why *are* you here?"

"I had no idea you would be here! I've come for a family reunion. The northern part of the family came south, and the southern part came north. I'm supposed to be with Dina—"

"Dina?"

"Dina Donatello, my cousin."

He stared at her for a moment as if he had been hit with a brick. Then he groaned and pressed his palm against his temple. "Joe's sister?"

"Yes!"

"Joe Donatello is your cousin?"

"Yes!" She felt as if they had been playing an absurd game of charades and he had finally figured out a tough word.

As if she had finally figured out a very tough word herself.

"Oh, no!" she gasped. "Joe's friend. You're Joe's friend. The one who owns the condo."

"Exactly," he murmured. His eyes were closed as he rubbed his forehead.

Lucia felt suddenly weak. She slid along the door until she was sitting against it. "Oh, no," she murmured. She should have known; she should have guessed. She had known that Ryan was from Massachusetts, and that he was a builder. But it had never occurred to her that he and Joe might know one another. Never.

He was staring at her again. She saw the suspicion in his expression even before he spoke. "You didn't know?"

"No, I didn't know."

"You just happened to stumble into my bed?"

"You idiot!" she snapped. "*Yes*, I just stumbled into your bed."

"With no idea?"

"Yes, with no idea!" She bounced to her feet, her pride intact. "And what about you, Mr. Dandridge? You know Joe—and you never heard about his cousin Lucia?"

"Joe has a dozen cousins."

"Two dozen, but so what? You planned this! Just what is it that you want? Are you trying to put me in a compromising position with my family, is that it? Make a fool out of me for walking out on the great Casanova?"

"Lucia, I never—"

"You're always—"

"You're a spoiled brat, Lucia. A spoiled little brat accustomed to getting your own way. Well, it doesn't always work like that in life."

Accustomed to getting her way...

She gritted her teeth. She didn't always get what she wanted. Not at all. She had wanted *him*. She had wanted a church wedding and flowers and a family and all the fixings of marriage. She had wanted the love to go on forever; she had wanted the tenderness and the laughter.

No, she didn't always get what she wanted.

"This is really your place?" she asked rigidly.

"Yes, Ms. Lorenzo, it is." He started to get out of bed. She remembered the way he looked. The way he walked.

"Don't!" she cried.

Startled, he looked her way. A lock of tawny hair fell over his eye, and he reached slowly for the sheet. As he rose, he wound it around his waist. She breathed more easily.

He opened a drawer in the bedside table and took out a pack of cigarettes and an ashtray. He lit a cigarette and blew smoke toward the ceiling.

"I thought you quit."

"I did." He paused. "Then I started again." He rose with the sheet still wrapped around him. He was still fabulous to look at. He had dropped out of school at sixteen to support his mother and his younger sisters. He had worked in construction, and his body attested to his labors.

His shoulders were heavily muscled and broad, his stomach was trim and flat, and his thighs and calves were heavily muscled. He was tall, so he appeared lean and sleek, but he was very powerful, and still graceful.

He moved to the rear of the room and pulled open the drapes. Sun poured through the glass doors that led to the balcony overlooking the beach and the Atlantic Ocean. He opened the door and walked out into the sunshine. He leaned on the wrought-iron railing, and Lucia saw his fingers grasp it tightly. He inhaled deeply on the cigarette, then irritably swung around and stared at her. "Joe's cousin. Fine. So what are you doing here?"

"Faith sent me here."

"Fate?"

"Faith! My Aunt Faith! Joe's mother." Lucia exhaled with aggravation. "My aunt assigned us singles—" She paused, sorry that she had used the term the second she saw his smirk. She lifted her chin and continued. "These are big condos, Ryan. They're mostly two- and three-bedroom places. Those of us who are unattached—" That word seemed to be even worse. "Aunt Faith was in charge of fitting us all in. This is where I was told to come."

She saw by the angle of his head that he was going to dispute her. "Damn you, Ryan, I'm telling you the truth."

"Sure."

"I am!"

"Like I said, sure."

She wanted to hit him, but that would mean touching him, and that was the one thing she couldn't let herself do. She clenched her hands into fists at her sides and swore instead, but she would rather have walked out onto the balcony and hit him.

"You set this up. I know it!" she said.

He started to laugh.

She couldn't help it. She walked across the room and out to the balcony. He warily tossed his cigarette into the large brass planter at his side, and she saw a curious sizzle rise to his eyes. He caught her wrists before she could slam her fists against his chest, and he pulled her taut against him. He was hot. Vital. His fingers wound tightly around her wrists.

"I swear," Lucia assured him, "I would rather crawl into bed with a porcupine! Or a rat—and that just might be pretty damn close—"

"Lucia, you're pushing it. Really pushing it. Is that what you want?"

He spoke tensely, in a whisper. His breath touched her cheek, and his tension seemed to become a part of her. Her blood leaped in her veins, and her heart beat raggedly, slamming against her chest. Her head was cast back so that she could meet his eyes. Snoopy and the sheet lay between them, but suddenly it seemed as if there were nothing at all, nothing but the sun, warm and sure and vibrant, shimmering down upon them, heating them.

She couldn't breathe. She couldn't speak.

"Lucia..."

He said her name softly, as he had that first night. As if he were tasting it. As if he found it very sweet.

She didn't know when he released her. Her hands were lying against his chest, and she felt the erratic movement of his heart beneath them. She felt his eyes staring into hers.

Then she felt his hands moving over her back. She was shivering, trembling, achingly aware of his touch. His fingers skimmed down the length of her spine to the small of her back and drew her closer. Closer...flush against him. Hip to hip. And still his fingers moved sensually over the curve of her buttocks, pressing her ever more tightly to him.

Then he moved his hand to her face and stroked his thumb gently over her cheek, gazing into her eyes. At last he lowered his head and kissed her.

His lips moved over hers, and she felt his tongue swiftly ravage her mouth. Reaching, exploring, plunging...delving. The air seemed to simmer. The heat entered her, swirled in her blood and shot to the core of her, and she trembled anew. No one could kiss as erotically as Ryan Dandridge. No one. No one could tell a woman so completely, just with the pressure of his lips, what he wanted, what he could give.

This was foolish, insane. She had to stop him.

She did nothing.

His left hand remained on the curve of her derriere, his right hand fell from her face, and he slowly lifted his lips from her mouth. His eyes, smoldering, were on hers.

"So this isn't what you came for, huh?"

She stiffened instantly, and he laughed delightedly at the fury her features betrayed. "Lucia—"

"Lucia! Are you up yet, dear?"

They both froze. It was Aunt Faith.

And apparently the front door to the apartment was open, because she heard Aunt Faith come right in. Staring at Ryan with high-school panic clearly written on her face, Lucia listened as Aunt Faith hummed away and turned on the coffee. "Lucia, did you make it?"

"Make what?" Ryan queried in a whisper.

"Shut up!" she returned in kind, kicking his shin.

"Ouch!"

"Shh!"

She felt his eyes on her, and she clenched her jaw tightly. She couldn't walk in there. Not now. She didn't know what to do. Aunt Faith wouldn't understand. She would never be able to explain.

Ryan was staring at her curiously. She realized for the first time that until now he really hadn't believed that she hadn't known he would be there.

"Aunt Faith?" he mouthed.

She nodded vigorously.

"Lucia, sweetie, are you here? Did you make it in okay? Dear, dear, dear, I knew she shouldn't have been driving all that way alone so late at night!"

Ryan smiled, watching Lucia. He shrugged. "Answer her. Tell her you'll be right out."

"Hi, Aunt Faith! I'm here!" she called. She kept staring at Ryan. Her hips were still flush with his, and his hand still rested on the curve of her buttocks.

"Oh, thank goodness!" Aunt Faith called back.

Then the bedroom door burst open and Aunt Faith rushed in. Tiny and pretty and dark-haired, with just a twinge of gray, she moved swiftly into the room with a broad smile on her face.

"Oh!"

There was silence among them.

Aunt Faith's smile faltered, then fell. She dragged it back into place, though it kept threatening to slip.

"Er, Lucia, dear, I'm so glad you made it! We were all worried, such a late drive, but you're here now and . . ." She paused, then cleared her throat. "And, well, I, er, I see that you and Mr. Dandridge have met."

Chapter 2

No! No, we haven't met!'' Lucia said quickly. Then she realized how absurd her words sounded and simply froze. They hadn't *met*? They were standing there intimately entwined, and he was still practically naked, and she was saying they hadn't even met! *Before*, that was what she had wanted to say. They hadn't met *before*. She had wanted to pretend that she didn't know Ryan Dandridge, that she had never seen him before in her life.

"Oh," Aunt Faith said.

It had to be one of the most awkward moments in Lucia's entire life. Though she had always prided herself on being in control in any situation, she had no control whatsoever then, with her Aunt Faith staring at her, stunned, her face as pale as a ghost's. For the life of her, Lucia couldn't think of a thing to say, not a single word to bail herself out of these miserable circumstances.

Ryan! It was all Ryan's fault! Just when she'd thought that she was straightening things out, he was back in her life, creating confusion and disaster. She fought daily to forget him, and now he was not only back, he was enmeshing her in an outrageous mess!

"Aunt Faith—"

"Mrs. Donatello," Ryan said smoothly, "this is awful, and it's absolutely not what it appears to be. I'm afraid that Joe made a mistake passing on the room arrangements. I've just met your niece in a rather awkward manner, I'm afraid. She wasn't expecting me, and I sure as he—er, I definitely wasn't expecting her."

"Oh," Aunt Faith said. It seemed to be all that she could manage to say herself. Her eyes were still wide, and Lucia thought that maybe she kept saying oh because her lips had frozen into that particular position.

"I came in so tired and so late that I just crawled into bed," Lucia said.

"Oh, dear," Aunt Faith murmured. Her lips had relaxed enough to let her form other words at last.

"I'd offered my penthouse to the girls," Ryan said. By now, Lucia realized, seeing him from the corner of her eye, he had managed to tie the sheet securely around his hips. "Maybe Joe didn't reach Ms. Lorenzo in time. Maybe he forgot. I'm not sure what happened. It seems to have been a little slip."

Aunt Faith tried to smile again. "Well, Lucia, dear, I'm just so glad to see that you made it in safely." She reached her arms out for a big hug, and Lucia stepped forward. Her aunt took her into a warm embrace, then whispered, "I'm so very glad, dear, that your mother isn't here." She hesitated. "And your father!"

At the moment Lucia was rather glad herself her father had taken her mother to Paris for their thirtieth wedding anniversary.

Ryan, clad in his sheet, swept by them both. He nodded to her and smiled to Aunt Faith. "If you'll excuse me, I'll solve some of this mess right now by dressing and going back to my own apartment. Ms. Lorenzo, it was a...pleasure. Mrs. Donatello, I'm very sorry for the discomfort this morning has caused you."

He might have been wearing a tux. Ryan had the ability to appear completely calm and totally authoritative no matter what he was wearing, a business suit, beach trunks, jeans...or a sheet over nothing at all. It was one of the things that had always irritated Lucia. The more excited she got, the calmer Ryan would be. It was impossible to win an argument with such a man.

It had been impossible to reach him, to know what he really thought, really felt, and whether or not he really cared at all, when she had been falling irrevocably in love.

Ryan escorted the two of them to the bedroom door and closed it. Lucia smiled weakly as she heard a drawer slam within the room.

"Lucia—" Aunt Faith said.

Lucia quickly hugged her. "Oh, Aunt Faith, it is so good to see you!"

She had to leave, Lucia realized. She couldn't stay here. Not if Ryan was going to be here. She had been looking forward to the comforting balm of her family, to forget the heartbreak and tempest of Ryan Dandridge. She didn't know how she was going to explain it to her aunts and uncles and cousins, but she was going to have to drive right back home. She couldn't stay in the same state with Ryan Dandridge.

The door burst open. Ryan, dressed in jeans and a T-shirt, stepped out. He excused himself politely to Aunt Faith, and stared at Lucia.

She stepped back quickly, letting him walk by. He looked good. His chest and shoulders were darkly bronzed from his time in the sun, and she wanted to reach out and touch him.

She clenched her fists. She'd already touched him once and been burned very badly in the process. This was a nightmare, and she had to wake up. This was her family reunion; how could he possible be a part of it?

"Faith, Mr. Dandridge," Aunt Faith was saying. "Please, no Mrs. this or that, I'm Faith."

He smiled, his heart-stopping, slow, easy smile. "All right, Faith. But no Mr. this or that, either, I'm just Ryan, okay?"

Aunt Faith grinned just like a high-school girl with an enormous crush. How quickly we all fall, Lucia thought acidly. She smiled herself. "Weren't you just leaving, Mr. Dandridge?"

Ryan arched a brow and walked on by. She watched as he moved down the hallway. She had to clutch the wall. She felt weak suddenly, and curious hot shivers sped over her flesh.

"Oh, Lucia, I'm so sorry!" Aunt Faith said.

"It's all right. It wasn't your fault."

"And he really is such a delightful man."

"Umm."

"You two got off on the wrong foot, I know, but the first time I saw him, I thought how charming he was and how right he might be for you."

"Aunt Faith, no matchmaking."

"No, no, dear, nothing like that. I wouldn't dream of actually matchmaking. He's just so good-looking."

Lucia smiled tightly. "Yes, he is."

"And he's such a hard worker. This place is his, you know. He's a builder. And he's doing very well."

"That's marvelous, Aunt Faith. I'm so very glad for him."

"He renovates old houses, too. With your love for old furniture and bric-a-brac—"

"Aunt Faith," Lucia interrupted with as sweet a smile as she could muster. She yawned widely. "Would you mind terribly if I went back to sleep for a while? It was such a long drive, and I'm afraid I got started very late."

"Of course not, dear," Aunt Faith began, but just then the outside door banged open and shut again as someone else came into the condominium.

"Lucia? You here?"

It was her cousin Joe, Aunt Faith's youngest son, and one of her closest friends since she had been a little girl. He came into the room with his dark flashing eyes and wide smile, and she forgot her misery for the moment, greeting him with a big hug. He squeezed her in return and went through a rapid-fire recital of all the usual questions: How was the drive? What time did she get in? Did she hit any bad weather? Didn't she just love the place? Wasn't it wonderful here? He didn't really wait for answers as he cast his arm around his mother's shoulders and said, "Isn't it just great to see her?"

"Of course!"

"I have a bone to pick with you, Joe," Lucia said severely.

"What?" He arched his brows innocently.

"There was a man in my bed this morning."

"Joe, it was just dreadful," his mother said. "How could you have done such a thing?"

"What do you mean?"

"There was a man in her bed," Aunt Faith said firmly. "Your friend Ryan. He said something about giving the penthouse to your cousins and that was why he was down here."

Joe slammed his palm against his forehead. "Oh, my God, I forgot. I completely forgot. Ryan did intend to let you and Dina use the penthouse."

"Then..." Lucia hesitated. "He knew I was coming?"

"He knew I had two single female cousins coming. And he's such a nice guy."

"A living doll," Lucia murmured.

"What was that, dear?" Aunt Faith said.

"Uh, nothing, nothing at all."

"Poor guy. He must have been as stunned as you were, Lucia."

"Was he?" she asked, wondering at his tone of voice.

"Lucia, he's my friend, but you were here, I wasn't."

"He seemed...surprised."

"Well, it couldn't have been too bad. You're both nice people, right?"

"Umm, sure."

"Dear, is something wrong?" Aunt Faith said.

"No, no, of course not."

Joe took her hands. "Lucia, I'm sorry. But Ryan is a real gentleman. Everything was all right, wasn't it?"

There was something odd about the way he was looking at her, Lucia thought. There seemed to be an extra light of mischief in his eyes. She had to be imagining things, she thought. He couldn't have meant to put her in such an awkward situation. Had he?

"Forgive me?"

"I—of course I forgive you."

"It's just that we're such a crowd. Ma and I had to make sure that the marrieds with children had enough room, and that the singles were with the singles, and, well, it can get confusing, you know?"

"Sure," Lucia said.

"Lucia wants to get a little more sleep, Joe," Aunt Faith told him. "Let's give her some privacy."

"Sure. Get some sleep, Lucia." Joe kissed her cheek. He was still looking at her in a curious fashion. "Go to sleep. We're going to have a big barbecue by the pool this evening. Everyone isn't going to want to do the same things every day, but we thought we'd start off tonight with hot dogs and hamburgers on the grill."

"Fine," Lucia murmured. "I'll be there."

Would she? She had a few things to say to Mr. Dandridge; then she would be on her way.

Aunt Faith gave her a fierce hug. "Oh, honey, we're so glad you could come! Georgia seems so far away. We're so grateful that we'll have this time together." She hugged Lucia once again, then stepped out of the condominium. Joe gave her a wry grin and a thumbs-up sign, then followed his mother out.

Lucia watched them go, feeling ill. She loved them all very much, and it *was* special to have this time together. She had always been grateful for her family. They were a big group, and confusion often reigned around them, but they were always there in a pinch, and no people in the world could be as loving and supportive. It was going to be difficult to leave.

Ryan! Damn him, this was simply impossible!

She didn't go back to sleep; she'd had no intention whatsoever of doing so. She threw her suitcase onto the bed and took out a bathing suit and a big overshirt. Then she walked into the bathroom for a shower, but found herself pausing instead.

Even the bathroom was nice. It was done in red and black and white, with a sheer glass shower stall and a red whirlpool tub that faced a little balcony with a garden. It was a functional bathroom, but it could also be very romantic.

She tossed her clothing on the floor and stepped into the shower stall. The water came out hot and strong. Standing beneath it, she prayed for calm and relaxation. She simmered and steamed instead, then sank down wearily to the floor and felt the water sting as it hit her flesh.

Walking out on him had been the hardest thing she had ever done in her life.

But it had been the right thing to do, she was certain. She had always said that any woman who stayed with a man who saw other women was a fool. She had been dreaming of a church wedding and her cousins

lined up as bridesmaids and ushers, but Ryan had
merely been passing the time.

A gentleman, Joe had said. Her cousin had called
Ryan Dandridge a gentleman.

In his way, maybe he was. Ryan opened doors; he
was courteous. He could also take what he wanted,
and he brooked no opposition. And once he had
wanted her. He had come after her with relentless de-
termination, and she had fallen. She'd never doubted
his intention of seducing her, nor had she ever under-
estimated his power to do so. His eyes alone could do
incredible things, seeming to touch her very flesh when
he looked at her. His kiss was full of sensual, intimate
promise. He bred the clouds of fantasy with his light-
est touch.

And he brought out the very worst in her, she reminded herself. She had never fought so terribly with
anyone else in her life. She had told herself that she
wouldn't cling, wouldn't be jealous, but he would stay
out too late, or receive a few too many telephone calls,
and she would find herself simmering inside. The ag-
ony of the wondering would make her ill. She would
go somewhere, anywhere, hoping that he would wonder and worry, too. And then the fights would start.
No, *she* would start them, because she didn't seem to
be able to help herself.

He never mentioned marriage, and he never mentioned commitment, and finally, when she realized
what she was doing, she made herself pick up and
walk away from it all. But she hadn't really left him,
not at all, because it felt as if she still slept with him
every night. He plagued her dreams relentlessly. He
interfered every time she met another man, because

she couldn't help comparing the two of them, and it seemed that every man came up lacking compared to Ryan Dandridge. It would change, she vowed to herself. All she had needed was time. Time to forget Ryan. And she could have done it, she could have. Except that he had walked back into her life at the most inappropriate time!

Lucia rose and turned off the water. She stepped out of the shower stall and briskly dried herself, then dressed, donning her swimsuit and the big white overshirt with the pink flamingos. She slipped into a pair of sandals and stormed out of the room. She wondered where her cousin Dina was. It didn't matter. She would see Dina and the others later, before she left. Unless she could convince Ryan Dandridge that *he* should leave.

She wanted to see the children, she thought. All her little second cousins. She wanted to see Theresa's and Bill's children; the baby would be three now, and Lucia hadn't seen her since she was nine months old. This wasn't fair. Not one bit. Damn Ryan Dandridge a thousand times over. She had twenty-five relatives here in this one spot, and the man was going to ruin her chance to enjoy their company.

As Lucia walked through the condo, she saw things she hadn't noticed when she had come in last night. The living room and dining room were combined, while the kitchen was separated by a wood block counter, with wonderful old-fashioned bar stools set in front of it. There was a coffee maker, and also a microwave, and the wallpaper had a country design. Large plate-glass windows gave way to a huge balcony that overlooked the Atlantic Ocean. There was a barbecue grill on the balcony, and a number of cushioned redwood chairs. The entire effect was very nice, and she bit her lip. Ryan was good, she thought grudgingly. Whether he restored an old single-family house or created a modern multifamily dwelling, he was good. He thought about the things that made a place convenient and comfortable, and also about the things that were artistic and pretty and pleasing to the eye. He was a talented man—in so many ways.

Swearing softly to herself, she turned and hurried out the door. She could hear sounds from next door, the apartment that Aunt Faith and Aunt Hope were sharing with their husbands. She could smell the delicious scent of broiling bacon. Her stomach growled softly, but she ignored it and looked down to the courtyard and pool below her second-floor terrace, then up to the floors that rose above her. The building was five stories tall, with parking underneath. The condos here all looked as if they had been built on stilts. It was to avoid flooding, she knew. Joe had told her so when he had given her directions to the place.

His "friend's" condo, where he had gotten such a wonderful deal for the family.

The condos were privately owned—by Ryan, she knew now:—and rented out as vacation apartments. They really were wonderful.

Damn Ryan.

Not at all sure what she could say or do to make the man leave, Lucia turned toward the elevator. Luckily, no one seemed to be out and about yet; she didn't see any of her relatives. They were all still inside their apartments having breakfast, or maybe some of them had already gone down to the beach. Her Uncle Paul loved the water. Whether they were in Maine or on the Cape or vacationing in Florida, Uncle Paul headed for the beach first thing. The children were probably already out, too.

Lucia stepped into the elevator and punched the button for the fifth floor. The elevator worked silently, and in a second the door opened. She just stared out for a moment. She was suddenly feeling cold and a little bit frightened, and she didn't know why.

Yes, she did. She shouldn't confront Ryan. She shouldn't even take the time to say goodbye to her family. She should hop into her car and drive as fast as she could toward home.

She stepped out of the elevator and walked determinedly toward the only door on the fifth floor. She raised her hand, then let it fall. She couldn't do it. She couldn't go through with it. She turned around, ready to go back downstairs.

The door was suddenly thrown open. Ryan was there, staring at her. She didn't like the hard glint in his eyes as he leaned against the door frame and smiled, crossing his arms over his chest. His chest was still bare, but he was wearing a pair of black bathing trunks with a little red insignia on the left leg.

"Were you coming to see me, Lucia?"

"No. I was lost."

He looked around inquiringly. "Lost, huh?"

"I pushed the wrong button on the elevator."

"You always were a rotten liar. So you were coming to see me, but you decided to run off without a word, instead. That does seem to be one of your best talents. Running, that is."

"I wasn't running."

"Yes, you were."

"I wasn't."

"Then come in."

She hesitated, stiffening. She had come up here to talk to him; she should do so, and then leave.

"Thank you."

She swept by him and into his penthouse apartment.

It was beautiful. The entry and the kitchen were bright and floored with marble tiles, and the living area was carpeted in cream. Colorful seascapes covered the walls, and the furniture was all of light pine, to accent the cool shades of the floors and walls. The rear of the apartment was glass overlooking the ocean, but the sheet glass doors went around to the side, too, overlooking the courtyard. The deep balcony went all the way around, and she saw comfortable furniture, a barbecue and a Jacuzzi surrounded by a wall on one side and foliage on the other. Very intimate and very private. She instantly wondered with whom he had shared the Jacuzzi, then hated herself for wondering. It wasn't her business anymore. It was over between them.

The door closed behind her. She started and turned around to see him looking at her grimly. "What's the matter, Ms. Lorenzo? Are you afraid to be with me?"

"Of course not."

"Just checking." He took a step toward her. She jumped back, and he laughed, walking into the kitchen. "Want some coffee?"

"No." It smelled wonderful, though. "Yes."

"Decisive. You know, I like that about you, Lucia."

"Don't be sarcastic."

"Why not? The situation demands it."

"You caused the situation."

"I did not."

"You knew I was coming here!"

Ryan poured out two cups of coffee and set the pot down. He automatically added one spoon of sugar to Lucia's, then left his own black. He looked at her over the counter. "Lucia, I had no idea that you were Joe's cousin."

"He's an Italian from Massachusetts!"

"Lucia, I'm willing to bet that there are at least a million Americans of Italian descent in Massachusetts." He shoved her coffee cup across the counter. "Besides which, you live in Georgia."

"But you knew that I had family in Massachusetts!"

"Lucia, I live in Massachusetts. That's why a lot of my friends are from there. And forgive me, but every time I meet someone with an Italian name, I don't ask if they happen to be related to you. Besides, I've known Joe a lot longer than I've known you."

"You have?"

"I have."

"You never mentioned his name."

"I probably never had a chance. You didn't stick around long enough. And neither did you—mention your cousin's name, that is."

She picked up her coffee and sipped it too quickly, lowering her eyes. She didn't know if he was telling the truth or not, but the large apartment suddenly seemed small. She shouldn't be here with him. From the moment they had first met, she had felt a dangerous attraction. She had wanted to touch him. And here he was in that skimpy bathing suit. It was too easy to remember the good times, the times when they had lain together and made love and laughed. Times when they had ordered pizza in the middle of the night, or gone for late walks in the snow and come in to be warmed by the fire. The good times... when she had allowed herself to trace patterns over his face with her fingertips, to explore the length of him. She wished fervently that they hadn't been so close, that intimacy had not come so easily to them. Then she wouldn't be standing here now, thinking that she hated him for being here, too, and simultaneously longing to go running into the kitchen, just to touch him again.

She didn't need to walk into the kitchen; he was walking out of it. He headed for the window overlooking the ocean and looked down at the water.

"You must have known!" she whispered.

He stared at her. He smiled, and a pulse beat quickly at his throat. "You know what I think, Lucia? I think *you* knew. I don't know what your game is yet, but surely Joe must have mentioned *my* name somewhere along the line. I've known him for years. Years and years. How do I know that you didn't know exactly what you were doing? Maybe you even went to Joe for help in getting close to me again. Maybe you walked out and then you just couldn't stand it—you had to get back into bed with me, so you arranged this whole thing."

She stood still for a minute, then exploded. "You idiot!" she accused him, and before she knew it, she was tearing across the apartment. She wasn't sure what she meant to do to him, whether she intended to toss her coffee on his chest or aim for his handsome but oh-so-smug features.

It didn't matter. He was ready for her. It was almost as if he had antagonized her on purpose. Before she knew it, the cup was plucked from her hand and she found her wrists clamped tight behind her at the small of her back. She stared up angrily into his eyes, demanding that he set her free instantly.

"What's the matter, Lucia, you didn't run fast enough this time?"

His face was so close that she could almost feel his freshly shaved cheeks. She wanted to lay her own face against the breadth of his chest.

It seemed that everything inside her was pounding like a massive drum, beating out a hot and deadly rhythm. Her flesh had come alive. She ached, and she realized bleakly that he was right. She did want to make love to him....

But she hadn't planned it! She hadn't planned any of it! All she wanted was for Ryan Dandridge to get out of her life.

"Why did you come here, Lucia?"

"Let me go."

"Answer me first. Why did you come here?"

"To ask you to go."

"What?"

"I want you to go. I want you to go back to Rhode Island or Massachusetts—or to Tombouctou. I don't care, just so long as you leave."

His face seemed to lose all its color. His hold on her wrists grew so tight that he hurt her, but she wouldn't let herself protest. "You're kidding."

"No, I'm not. I'm begging. Please, Ryan. This is important to us, to all of us. I don't get to see my family that often, now that I live in Atlanta. Please try to understand, I want to see my family."

"Who's stopping you?"

"You are!"

"I'm not!"

"You're here!"

"I own this place!"

"Yes, but—"

"Lucia, you're not being reasonable."

"I want—"

"You want, you want. Same old story, isn't it? You never were reasonable. I don't know why I should expect you to start now."

"Ryan, if you don't leave, I will."

"Right. Run again. You handle things so well. What are you afraid of, Lucia?"

"I'm not afraid of anything!"

"Then why are you running?"

"Oh!" She tugged hard on her hands, desperate to escape his hold. She could feel his flesh burning through the thin material of her T-shirt, and her breasts were hard against the wall of his chest. They were far too intimate.

"Ryan Dandridge—"

"Why did you run away, Lucia?"

"Ryan, it wasn't working out—"

"Why?"

"Would you please let me go?"

"Why? So you can take a swing at me again?"

"Let me—" She tried to kick him.

"Hey!" he protested, and before she knew it, he had set a foot behind her ankles and she was tumbling to the floor, with him on top of her. She struggled in silence, but he straddled her and caught her hands, lacing his fingers through hers.

"Lucia, you have one of the worst tempers I have ever encountered."

"It's only my reaction to your conceit!"

"Well, try this on for conceit. I'm not changing my plans for your convenience, Ms. Lorenzo. You've already put a few dents in my armor. I'm not going to let you do it again. Got it?"

"Ryan—"

"So what are you going to do?"

He was too close, and she was far too vulnerable. She could feel the callused pads of his fingers and, despite herself, she remembered how erotic they felt moving lightly over her bare flesh. She felt the muscled tightness of his thighs, and saw the blue fever in his eyes. She didn't want him touching her . . . because he had touched her too often in the past, and the past was gone.

"I am going to leave."

He let out a sound of disgust. "Coward," he said softly.

"Damn you, Ryan."

"I'll tell you what, Lucia. I won't leave, but I will promise you this—I'll do my best to avoid you. How's that?"

"I don't—"

"I'll stay away from you. This isn't a huge place, but I'm sure we won't run into one another that often. Then, if you've got any guts at all, you can stay."

She felt her breath coming too fast as she stared up at him. For a moment they were both silent. She started to tremble, and she hated herself for it. She always gave away too much of her emotions. Ryan was always in control, cool and hard; he gave away nothing.

"Ryan..."

"You think I can't stay away from you, Lucia, is that it? You know, the first time I saw you, I *couldn't* stay away. I never wanted a woman so badly in my entire life. I never saw eyes so dark, or hair so glossy. The second I looked at you, I was trapped. I had to stare again and again. You were the most beautiful and absolutely sensual woman I had ever seen."

He lowered himself slowly against her. He came so close that his mouth was just half an inch from hers, so that the whisper of his words caressed her cheeks and teased her lips.

"I had to meet you, Lucia. I just had to meet you. And then, when I got close, I found out that I liked everything about you. I liked the way you were so indignant at first. I liked the way you handled yourself. I liked the scent of your perfume, and I was in love with the flash in your eyes. That very moment, I was hot and desperate, and I wanted you."

Closer, closer he came, until the movement of his lips as he spoke was something that she could feel.

"I liked your voice and your laughter and the way you tossed your head when you were excited. I liked the feel of your hair, and the brush of your fingers, and the closer we got, the more I liked, the more I needed, the more I had to have. Lucia, you've got beautiful skin, and a beautiful sway to your hips, and the most beautiful breasts...."

She hadn't even realized that he had let go of her wrists, but suddenly his hands were on her. Through the T-shirt and her bikini top, his fingers caressed and cradled the fullness of her breast, and the sensation, after so much time, was shocking. It made her warm, and then it made her hot and trembling and frightened, all at the same time. She had to stop him.

"Ryan..."

His lips came down on hers in a kiss that was strong and passionate. She didn't even think to protest.

It felt so good, so right.

His mouth covered hers firmly and persuasively. His tongue plundered its way inside, demanding more, and then more. By the time she did think to protest, his lips were locked with hers, fervent and wet and demanding, and his tongue was stroking the soft inner flesh of her mouth. Feelings erupted inside her, sweeping down the length of her. It had always been like this. No matter how angry she was, he had only to touch her, and she didn't care about anything except her need to be with him. His kiss awoke passion and hunger. She wanted to thread her fingers into his hair, to take more and more of him. She wanted to arch against him and move her fingers over the bare wall of muscle on his chest. She wanted to stroke his back and tenderly touch his cheeks and breathe the scent of him forever....

Damn him!

What was he doing to her? She had left him once, and she had learned slowly and painfully how to live without him. She had to stop him now, before she forgot those hard-learned lessons. She had to escape!

Suddenly she didn't need to. He lifted his face from hers, slowly breaking the kiss, breaking the sweet contact between them. She stared at him, longing to tell him that she hated him, but the words wouldn't come. Her lips were wet from his, and he was still pressed against her intimately.

"Lucia, I was desperate for you then. And do you know what? I still think you have wonderful, expressive eyes. I still think you're beautiful. You have the softest flesh and the most tempting lips in the entire world." He paused, sighing softly. "But . . ."

He smiled and sat away from her, though he was still straddling her. "But I *can* control myself. I can promise to stay away from you. Can you really promise to keep your hands off me?"

Lucia emitted a sound of pure rage, instinctively striking out to dislodge him. He laughed and caught her wrists again. "Hey! Calm down, Ms. Lorenzo."

"If you have such great control, get off me right now!"

Still holding her wrists and keeping a wary eye on her, he stood, then moved to help her to her feet. She was so determined not to accept his help that she only stood up when he literally dragged her into position.

"Uh-uh, control, Ms. Lorenzo!" he said, laughing.

"Control? You talk about control after all the things you did?"

"But I didn't walk out in the middle of the night, Lucia. No word, no explanation. You're the one who did that." He was still holding her warily, but his laughter was gone. His words were soft, but somehow dangerous.

"Ryan..."

"I'll let you go. But do yourself a favor this time, Lucia. Don't run."

He released her, and she stood dead still, her fists clenched, her jaw locked, shaking. She stared at him, seething, yet all she could think of was a single word. "Idiot!" she raged, then spun around, heading for the door.

"Nice to see you, too, Lucia."

There was a pillow on the sofa. She picked it up and hurled it his way with the force of a military missile.

He caught it and laughed softly. "Temper, Lucia. Watch that temper. Calm down before you start driving. You can be dangerous when you're in that mood. Believe me, I know, and I wouldn't want to have an accident on my conscience."

"You don't need to worry about it. You have nothing to do with me at all. I'm not even angry anymore. And I'm not driving anywhere," she lied. She was more than angry; she was livid. She was so furious that she was afraid she would pull the door right off its hinges when she tried to leave.

"You're not?"

"No, I'm not."

"You're not running?"

"I never did run, I walked."

"I thought you were going back to Atlanta."

"No, Ryan, I'm not going anywhere. I guarantee I can keep my hands off you. You're the one with the problem."

"Oh, I don't know. You are quite beautiful, but then, other women come with the same basic equipment. Maybe not as good as yours, but passable..."

She paused at the door, pulling her anger tightly under control, then smiled at him as sweetly as she could. "Other men come with equipment, too, Mr. Dandridge. And who knows? It just might be better than yours..."

Still smiling sweetly, she watched rage darken his features, and something inside her exulted. She had made him mad; she'd really gotten to him. She'd hurt him right in the ego, she thought happily.

It felt good. She threw open the door and walked out of his apartment.

"Lucia!"

She slammed the door and, smiling, headed for the elevator.

Chapter 3

Down at the beach, Lucia found her cousin Theresa, her husband Bill and their four children. Jimmy and Giles were ten-year-old twins, eternally precocious. Serena was eight, and an eternal plague, according to the twins. Tracy, the baby, had turned three. Lucia was Tracy's godmother, and although she was crazy about all the children, it was the baby she'd been longing to see.

Tracy, in a little blue bikini, was running back and forth to the water's edge, laughing with delight as the waves came in and out. The boys saw Lucia and came running to hug her. They had reached the squirming age, she realized when she tried to kiss them in return. They wouldn't hold still for kisses anymore. Serena would, though. Blushing and happy, she attached herself to Lucia. Tracy wandered over on her chubby little legs and went into gales of laughter when

Lucia kissed and hugged her. Finally she made it to
Bill, one of her very favorite in-laws, and then her
cousin, Theresa.

"Lucia, we're so glad you could come!" Theresa
assured her.

"It's been too long," Bill agreed, sitting beside his
wife and casually casting an arm over her shoulder.

"And isn't this glorious?" Theresa waved to indicate the shimmering Atlantic, the warm sand and the
brilliant sun. "It's just wonderful."

"It's hot," Tracy complained.

"Hey! There's Dina!" Theresa said, jumping to her
feet.

They went through the whole thing again, everyone
kissing everyone and laughing happily. Dina, Joe's
sister and Aunt Faith's youngest daughter, was, Lucia had always thought, one of the most beautiful
women she had ever met. Her eyes were huge and lu-
minous, their color a fascinating shade between blue
and gray, and her hair was nearly jet black. Lucia had
once heard that it was impossible for hair to be really
black; if that was so, Dina had the closest thing Lucia
had ever seen. Dina's hair was short and sleek and
scissor cut, and it fell in soft curls around her face.
Dina was fun to be with, too. She was totally irrever-
ent about almost everything, and knew how to tease
her mother and her aunts mercilessly. She loved to
dance and to party, and in general—though she was
very selective when it came to her intimate relations—
she loved men.

"Lucia, Lucia, ooh, I'm so glad you decided to
come! I hated the idea of spending the entire time with
my brother."

"Poor Joe." Bill sighed.

Dina kicked him. "What fun could I possibly have out with my brother all of the time?"

"Well, there's us, you know."

"Staid marrieds."

"I resent that!" Theresa protested.

"Well, you have the kids—"

"Yeah, and just for that, you're going to get to baby-sit one night," Theresa assured Dina.

"We're too old for baby-sitters!" Jimmy protested.

"Okay, Auntie Dina can brat sit, then," their mother warned them, moving her mirrored sunglasses down her nose so the boys could get a good look at the threat in her eyes.

"Dina, Dina!" Tracy said, racing over to this new cousin.

Lucia started to laugh. "Dina and I promise to give you two a few nights. You can go out somewhere wonderfully romantic and come back when the sun is rising, how's that?"

"Sounds great," Bill said, offering her a smile that said thank you beautifully.

"With my luck, I'll just get pregnant again," Theresa said, sighing. "Still, it really is great to be here all together, huh?"

"Yes, it is. It's great," Lucia agreed. She nuzzled little Tracy's brown curls and thought that it was darned good to be together, and that she wasn't going to let Ryan Dandridge ruin a single minute of it.

"Hey!" Dina, who'd been sprawled out in a skimpy white bikini that did great things for her lithe, tanned body, suddenly sat up. "My God, it's Ryan, isn't it?"

Little trickles of anxiety rippled along Lucia's spine.

Dina was right. It *was* Ryan, far down the beach. He stopped to talk to a man and a woman stretched out on beach chairs with drinks in their hands, then started toward the water again. He looked great, Lucia thought. As if he had been created to wear swim trunks and run along the sand. He was dark and athletic, and even on a beach filled with handsome men, he drew attention and then admiration.

Lucia thought Dina was going to purr. "I haven't seen Ryan in a long time. Not in a long, long time."

"But you know him?" Lucia said.

Dina cast her a quick, sharp gaze. "Sure I know him. He and Joe have been friends for years. Have you met him yet?"

"Yes."

"Kind of makes your tongue hang out, doesn't he?" Dina said cheerfully.

"Well, I don't know," Lucia said.

"Oh, Lucia!" Theresa laughed.

"And what's the matter with me?" Bill asked his wife.

"Nothing, sweetheart, nothing. He's just—well, he's still got all his hair. Maybe that's it."

Dina and Lucia both started to laugh; then Bill joined in and worriedly fingered the thinning strands on top of his head. Theresa assured him that she had always thought of Yul Brynner as an incredibly sexy man. Then she threw her arms around him, sending him crashing into the sand. "I love you, no matter what, I promise."

A moment later the kids fell over the two of them, and then everyone got in on the act, and they were all laughing, with sand in their mouths and in their eyes.

Sobering, Lucia realized that this was why she had left Ryan, that the special thing that Theresa and Bill shared was what she wanted. The children, the laughter, the happily-ever-after kind of love. Ryan was striking and hard and fascinating; he was rich color and tremendous passion, but she was certain that he couldn't be harnessed and held.

And she couldn't let herself love him, because the two of them couldn't have that special something she had always believed to be right. She had loved him with all her heart, and she had dreamed of marriage and kids and the works. She had lived her life believing in love and commitment; she couldn't change things now.

"Hey, how about lunch up at our apartment?" Theresa suggested. She made a face. "Hot dogs and chips, but lots of cold beer and coolers."

"It sounds great," Lucia said. She swept Tracy into her arms, and rescued a crab from Jimmy's fascinated scrutiny. "Lunch, guys. We'll come back down later."

Theresa and Dina gathered up the blankets, the sun block, the pails and T-shirts, and they all headed toward the elevator. A strange feeling teased the back of Lucia's neck, making her pause and look back, like Lot's wife.

Ryan was just coming out of the water. His eyes fell on her, and he set his hands on his hips, droplets sluicing over his chest and down his long, hard thighs.

"Hi, Ryan!" Tracy called.

Ryan waved to her.

"Come to lunch?" Tracy demanded.

Ryan shook his head, and his eyes met Lucia's. "Some other time!" he promised Tracy. Then his eyes skimmed Lucia's form, from the top of her head to her bare, sandy feet, and she felt suddenly naked. She was barely clad to begin with and, of course, he knew what lay beneath the little bit she was wearing. Despite herself, she began to flush, and she turned around very quickly.

She wondered just how well Dina had known Ryan, and no matter how she fought it, she was jealous.

After lunch Theresa decided that since Tracy wanted a nap, she was going to take one herself. Lucia thought that a nap sounded good, considering that she'd gotten very little sleep the night before. Dina and she walked the few steps to their own condominium. "Joe and Al are going to be right above us. Aunt Faith and Aunt Charity are next door. Hope and Paul are upstairs, and they're going to have Frank and Ellen and the kids. Of course, they're hardly kids anymore, since they're both in college."

"I know. It seems time really flies, doesn't it?"

Dina nodded. "I can't believe that Ellen and Frankie have grown kids. Did they start really early, or are we starting really late?"

Lucia laughed. "Frank is twelve years older than you are and fourteen years older than me."

Dina shrugged, walking into the condo and casually tossing her beach bag onto the couch. "Lucia, do you know that I'll be thirty next month?"

"Yes. Are you hinting around for a present or a sympathy card?"

Dina wagged a finger at her. "Go ahead, laugh. You're right behind me, and you won't be so amused if you get to my age without being—"

"Married?" Lucia said, startled that Dina would say such a thing. Dina Donatello had been at the top of her class in high school and again in college. She had a thriving design studio of her own in Boston. Over the years, Lucia had often done furniture restorations for her cousin's clients, and she had always been convinced that nothing would ever mean more to Dina than her business.

Dina shrugged. "It's funny, isn't it? I watched Ellen and Theresa and the others with their kids. I watched them sit home without two cents to rub together, worrying about bottles and diapers, and I thought I didn't want any part of it, not a bit. Now, all of a sudden, I do want a family. I want a little cherub just like Tracy, or a little lady like Serena, or even a pair of scamps like those twins. And I'm wondering if it isn't too late."

"Dina, it's never too late."

"Don't kid yourself. It can be too late. Anyway, this year I'm going to start concentrating on finding the right guy, and when I do find him, I intend to latch on—hard. I suggest you do the same thing."

"Dina, I don't think I was actively avoiding the right guy to begin with," Lucia told her cousin. She hesitated, and Dina gave her a stricken look. Lucia had been married once, long ago, when she had gotten out of high school. It had been a disaster; both of them had been far too young for marriage, and she had gone through a long and painful annulment for her parents' sake. "I—I just don't want to make a mistake again, that's all. I want someone who loves me as much as I love him, someone who wants the commitment of marriage as much as I do." She sat down and hugged a pillow to her chest. "Someone who wants children."

Dina stood up, smiling again, ever the optimist. "Well, we'll work on that as soon as we get back to our normal lives. While we're here, let's party. What's the nightlife like?"

Lucia laughed. "I've never been here before. We'll have to explore and find out. But not tonight. The Three Graces have planned a barbecue by the pool."

"Oh, no. Mother has been at it again." Dina groaned.

"It's the first night. It's a great idea for us all to be together."

"Okay. But if we survive the first three hours, we get to head out, what do you say?"

Lucia yawned and promised that they would go out. Dina headed down the hall. "Hey!" she called out. "What luxury!"

"What are you talking about?"

Dina reappeared in front of her. "There are *two* bedrooms here. One for you, one for me!"

"What?" Lucia felt crimson color come to her face. *Two* bedrooms. And she had crawled in with Ryan. "What?" she repeated, jumping up.

"Lucia, you're all flushed. You need some rest."

"I'm fine!" She wasn't fine. She was humiliated, but, thankfully, Dina didn't pursue the subject.

"My own room? Not that I mind sharing with you, but I do love space! I'm off!" Dina called.

Lucia didn't bother to go to her room. She flopped down on the couch, stuffed a pillow behind her head and lay there burning with embarrassment until, finally, she fell asleep.

Somewhere in the middle of her nap she began to dream. Ryan was in her dream, which, even in the dream, didn't surprise her very much. He had never been far from her thoughts, and now she had seen him again, so he was dead center in her mind, and in her heart.

He was on the beach, wearing the same black swim trunks he had worn that morning. He had already been in the water, and he was walking toward her purposefully, and though he didn't smile, there was a devilish light in his eyes that made her grow warm inside, the bold, blatant, sexual stare that never failed to send her senses reeling. The sun was hot, gleaming down on her, and they were all alone on the beach. The sound of the pounding surf cascaded all around them, and she knew that she was waiting, just waiting for him to come to her again. In a moment she would rise. She would stretch out her arms to him. She would rise, wet and sleek herself from the surf, and she would cry out and run into his arms....

"Ryan!"

Her cousin Dina's deep, sultry voice entered her dream from somewhere behind her. "Ryan, it's so nice to see you."

Ryan wasn't coming at her at all. He was running right past her open arms, as if he hadn't even seen her. He was turning his hungry stare on Dina. He was reaching out for Dina. Taking Lucia's beautiful and dazzling cousin into his arms.

"No, no, come in! I saw you on the beach. Ryan, it's been ages!"

Lucia started and realized that her cousin's voice wasn't coming from her dream at all. Dina was at the door to the condo—and Ryan Dandridge really was in her arms.

Dina kissed and hugged him effusively, but when he kissed and hugged her back, it was difficult for Lucia to tell whether he was just as effusive. He was trying to talk as she greeted him.

"I came up for your mother. She said the two of you were late, that they already had the burgers on the barbecue, and that you were to come down right now."

"Okay, we're coming. You going to be there?"

Lucia managed to sit up. She was still in her swimsuit, and her hair had dried like a giant hedge. She was certain that she looked like something the swamp creature had dragged in.

Ryan looked past Dina, right at her. She stared at him, dazed.

"I, er, I wasn't really planning on coming down," he said.

"But you have to!" Dina must have sensed that Lucia had awakened. She turned around, saw Lucia and laughed. "You two have met, right? Help me! Convince Ryan that he just has to come downstairs and join the barbecue."

Lucia tried to smile. She was certain the effort resembled a snarl.

"I'll see. Excuse me," Ryan told Dina before Lucia had a chance to speak.

Dina must have looked crushed, because Ryan tilted her chin up and smiled. "I'll see, okay, kid?" He kissed her forehead, then turned and walked away.

Dina grinned at her cousin. "Now *that* could be the right man."

"You think so? I had the impression he wasn't interested in settling down."

"I didn't realize you knew him that well."

"I—I don't." She felt terrible. She hated to lie. She just couldn't explain the whole truth of her relationship with Ryan, so she was tripping over lie after lie. "I just got the impression that he liked to—that he liked to move, I guess. That he wasn't interested in anything permanent."

Dina smiled, looking like a tigress, and fluffed up her hair. "Sometimes a man needs to be convinced that he wants to settle down. We'll see. Come on, come on, come on! We're late, and hail, hail! The gang's all here, and the barbecue is on. Let's go."

"I look like a drowned rat."

"I'll push you into the pool the moment we get downstairs and no one will ever know the difference."

Dina was one to talk. She had taken a shower, put on a new bathing suit, repaired her makeup and blow-dried her hair.

"Give me a minute," Lucia said dryly. "I'll try a brush first, okay?"

"Whatever you say."

Ten minutes later they were down by the pool. Everyone was there: her three aunts and her three uncles; Theresa and Bill and their children; Ellen and Frank with Katie and Bryce; Joe and Al; Theresa's brother Johnny and his wife Sophie, their son Mark, and their new baby, Valerie; and Frank's brother, Leon, who was Lucia's exact age and another of her favorite relatives.

The first twenty minutes were spent indulging in more hugs and kisses, until everyone had had a chance to hug and kiss everyone else, comment on the sizes of the children and kiss and hug each other all over again. It was wonderful, and it was warm, and Lucia was suddenly grateful with all her heart that she hadn't driven away—even if she was going to be tortured by Ryan Dandridge and her own cousin Dina for the duration.

"If only your mother were here!" Aunt Faith said to Lucia.

Uncle Mario, turning burgers on the barbecue, winked at her. "And your father."

Lucia smiled in return.

"Patience should be here," Aunt Charity said. "And Henry, too, of course." She smiled brilliantly, then beamed at her nephew Frank, sitting with Ellen. "Isn't he a handsome young man!"

Frank's mother, Hope, ruffled his hair. "A very handsome young man."

"Ma, I'm forty-four, balding, and I have two kids in college," Frank said with good humor, grimacing to his cousins. They all laughed because they all understood. To the Three Graces—and Patience, too—they were all always going to be young and handsome or beautiful, and brilliant, too, of course.

Aunt Hope appealed to her daughter-in-law. "Isn't he a handsome young man?"

"He's a charmer, Mom, a pure charmer."

They all laughed again. Mark, the twins and Serena headed for the pool, and Uncle Mario started handing out plates. It was late afternoon, and though the sun was very strong and the heat was tremendous, there was just enough of a breeze to make it nice. Lucia insisted on taking Valerie so Sophie could eat, and while she was asking about her newest relation's weight and length and sleeping habits, Aunt Faith's voice suddenly rose above all the chatter. "Where is that nice young man?"

"Which nice young man?" Frank said. "You mean me? No, I'm the handsome young man, right?"

"Right," Bill quipped.

Aunt Faith cast them both one of her chastising frowns. "Ryan Dandridge. We invited him, and he said he would come."

Lucia tensed, squeezing the baby too tight, and was instantly remorseful when Valerie looked up at her with innocent blue eyes, quivered her little lips and started to cry.

Dina jumped up. "I'll go drag him down. Be right back."

Lucia tried to soothe the baby. Faith and Hope announced that the next night was going to be pasta night. "Homemade ravioli and cappelletti, eggplant and sausage."

"For all of us?" Theresa asked.

"For everyone. Then we'll all be on our own for meals. But one pasta night with the family..." She shrugged. "We have to have one pasta night."

"Here he is!"

Dina's voice broke cheerfully through the noise. She had reappeared with Ryan Dandridge on her arm and a beautiful smile on her features.

Ryan looked decidedly uncomfortable, but Aunt Faith didn't notice, or, if she did, she wasn't going to acknowledge it. "Ryan! You promised that you would come right back! Dinner has been on for quite a while. Frankie, give Ryan a beer. Mario, fix him a plate. Come on, Ryan, now *mange, mange!*"

It was impossible not to obey Aunt Faith without being entirely rude. In a matter of seconds Ryan had a plate piled high with a huge burger and cold tortellini salad. There were people spread out all over the lounges and chairs at the poolside, and Lucia realized too late that the seat next to her at the redwood table was empty.

"Sit, eat. *Mange!*" Uncle Mario insisted. "You know my niece Lucia, Ryan? Lucia, Ryan, Ryan, Lucia. Now is that a beautiful girl, or what, eh, Ryan?"

Ryan's eyes fell on Lucia. She knew that she must have been a thousand shades of red. "That's a beautiful girl," he said softly.

Someone popped the top of a beer can as it was set before Ryan. Lucia started to jump to her feet. "Excuse me, I'll just go get myself a—"

"You've got the baby, you sit," Aunt Hope said. "What do you want, Lucia? I'll get it for you."

She felt Ryan smiling, just as she felt the muscled heat of his thigh next to hers, and every movement of his arm.

She looked at him, patting the baby on the back, then smiled, and allowed her leg to touch his. She could play the game, too.

"A cooler, Aunt Hope. I'd love one of those wine coolers, please."

Ryan smiled. The game was on.

Sophie came back and retrieved the baby. Theresa suggested a game of goony golf, and Aunt Hope said that she would take care of the children—all of them.

"All six?" Frank laughed.

Katie said she would stay at the condo and help, and Frank asked about taking a ride down to see Charleston one day during their stay.

Lucia didn't say a word. She sat there silently and smiled now and then. Ryan was dragged into the various conversations. All the aunts had to thank him again for the reasonable rates they had been given, and for being allowed to take over the pool area. Joe talked to him about building codes, and Theresa asked him about the area.

Lucia never forgot that she was sitting next to him, but somewhere along the line, she stopped paying attention to the conversation, because a newcomer joined their group.

She stiffened the minute she saw him, a short, dark, portly man, talking to her Uncle Mario by the barbecue pit. He had a smile that looked as if a snake was slithering across his face.

His name was Gino Lopez.

Gino was a loan shark who had done very well with his business. She had met him when she was very young, when they had been up north visiting for the summer. Her father had borrowed money from Gino, and had lived to regret taking the easy way out of his financial difficulties. Almost all her family had been suckered in by him at one time or another. What was he doing here?

Lucia felt Ryan move beside her, following her gaze.

"Lopez," he said softly.

Lucia stared at him hard. "You know him?"

"You keep forgetting—I live in Boston. Yes, I've had occasion to meet Gino Lopez."

"What's he doing here?"

"I don't know."

Theresa suddenly inhaled sharply. "He's getting into a fight with Uncle Mario, that's what he's doing. Bill?" she appealed nervously to her husband.

It seemed to be true. Uncle Mario was starting to look flushed and angry. Lopez was still smiling his oily smile, and talking away.

Lucia's uncles, Paul and Tony, got up and went over to the two men. The voices were still inaudible, but the anger was growing.

Ryan gripped Lucia's shoulder. "Is something going on here?"

"Is something going on? No! Don't you dare insinuate things. Just because we're Italian—"

"I'm not insinuating anything. And you don't have to be Italian to be suckered in by Lopez. I was just asking, that's all."

"There is nothing going on," Lucia grated out.

"Fine," Ryan said.

He stood up and approached the group of men. "Gino!" His voice rang out loudly, and he stuck out a hand, capturing that of the portly intruder. "What a surprise. I didn't know you were coming down. Where are you staying?''

Lucia didn't hear the answer. She did see that Ryan managed to separate Gino Lopez from her uncles and steer him toward the gate in the fence that surrounded the pool area. She was sure that Lopez himself didn't know what was happening, but in a matter of moments he was on the other side of the gate, cordially being locked out.

And then, a few moments later, Ryan was back beside Lucia.

"What is he doing here?" she asked. Theresa, troubled, was staring at the two of them.

Ryan shrugged. "I don't know."

"Maybe he's just down for the beach. This is becoming a very popular vacation spot, right?"

Ryan shrugged again. He saw the worry on Theresa's pretty face. "He could be down here for any number of reasons. I'm not the only New England builder working in this area. Half of these new places have been built by northern interests. Don't worry. He's not staying here—he told me that he and his son are at another condo north of here, closer to Myrtle Beach. If he were after someone here—"

"Why would he be after someone here?" Lucia exploded.

"Lucia, don't be so sensitive," Theresa said.

"Maybe he isn't after anyone at all," Ryan said. "Maybe he's just on vacation, soaking up some sun. Anyway, Theresa, please don't worry."

Theresa smiled, reaching across the table to squeeze his hand. "Thanks, Ryan. I won't."

A startled scream suddenly attracted their attention. Giles had tossed Jimmy into the pool. He came up sputtering, promising Giles that he would pay. Giles was already paying because his father had come up behind him and tossed him into the pool, too. Then Joe sneaked up behind Bill and shoved *him* in. "Excuse me," Ryan said suddenly, and he rose, shoving Joe from behind. With his arms flapping and waving madly, Joe pitched forward into the pool.

And then Ryan was just there...standing right at the edge of the nice, big, deep, sparkling clear pool. He watched as Giles tried to dunk Joe, his hands casually on his hips, his whole manner relaxed.

Lucia should have resisted the temptation. She really should have. But she couldn't. He was standing there too temptingly.

She leaped up with a quick shrug for Theresa and went racing over the cool deck to Ryan. He started to turn, but not in time. She caught his broad back with both her palms. For a moment he stared at her with amazement, faltering, swaying backward and forward.

Then his eyes narrowed briefly with the promise of revenge, and he flopped over backward, crashing into the water.

Lucia held still for a minute, watching him sputter to the surface. His eyes met hers as he swam toward the side of the pool.

There was laughter all around them. The tension that had come with Gino Lopez's appearance had faded away, and they were all having a good time. It was all good clean fun—except for the way that Ryan was looking at her....

Lucia let out a little yelp and decided to make a run for it. She spun around and wondered where to go. Her only choice was over the fence and down the beach. She turned around. Ryan was almost over the side.

"Run, Lucia, run!" Giles warned her.

"You'll never make it!" Mark called.

She didn't know if she would make it or not, but she pelted over the fence and tore down the beach.

Night was coming on. The horizon was gold and pink and crimson, and the tide was high. The scenery was glorious, with the waves turning to tiny white-caps, and the breeze salty and sweet.

Lucia barely noted the beauty as she ran. The water splashed beneath her feet, and her muscles quickly knotted. She turned her head.

Ryan was gaining on her.

Surf and sand were flying up behind him, and every long stride brought him closer. It wasn't fair. He was taller, and his legs were longer. He was coming closer every minute. He was almost on top of her.

"No!" Lucia shrieked. She turned, running into the deeper water. It slowed her down, but it slowed him down, too. She spun around, backing away, then yelling at him. "You're supposed to be able to keep your hands off me, remember?"

There was a wolfish look in his eyes. "You touched me first. Any time you can't keep your hands off of me, I get a freebie."

"What?"

"I didn't start it. You did. And I get to end it!"

She couldn't keep running. She could barely breathe. But he was still coming after her, so she be-

gan staggering back to shore. The water was warm and
dark. She stepped on a shell and winced, then lost
valuable time as she favored her wounded foot.

She realized that half the family had come out on
the beach.

"Come on, Lucia, run!" Theresa laughed.

"She'll never make it!" Mark prophesied.

"Come on, dear!" Aunt Faith encouraged her.
"Run!"

She cleared the water and started running again. She
heard the fury of his swift footsteps behind her; then
the air was knocked cleanly from her as Ryan swept
her off her feet and heaved her over his shoulder.

"How can you do this to me? In front of my whole
family?" Lucia gasped.

"Aren't you glad your mother isn't here?" he
taunted.

"You better be glad that my father isn't here!" Lucia threatened.

Ryan started to laugh. She swung against him,
tasted the salt on his back and felt the wet sleek
warmth of his body. He was holding her thighs, very
close to the rounded curve of her derriere. She
shouldn't have touched him, because now he was
touching her. And the others were all laughing and
having a good time, thinking that it was all such good,
harmless, clean fun....

And it wasn't that at all. It was painful to be held
this way, because it made her want so much more.
Because it brought back so many memories.

"Oh!" She screamed as she suddenly went flying,
then slammed into the cool water of the pool and
sank. When she came sputtering to the surface, her

male cousins were all cheering Ryan on, and even Theresa and Dina and Sophie were laughing.

Gasping for breath and treading water, Lucia stared at Ryan. The shadows of the coming night hid his features, and she couldn't see his eyes as he looked at her, his arms crossed over his chest.

Then he jumped into the water and started swimming toward her.

"No!" she gasped. Jimmy was still in the water. Lucia grabbed her cousin and pushed him toward Ryan. "Do something! Stop him."

"Do what, Lucia?" Jimmy demanded.

"I don't know."

Ryan surfaced. Jimmy giggled and plunged after him. "Oh, no, have mercy!" Ryan pleaded.

Jimmy went into gales of laughter. Ryan allowed Jimmy to dunk him; then he lifted him high out of the water and sent him diving back in.

Then his eyes fell on Lucia again.

"Get her, tiger!" Joe called out.

"Joe, damn you!" Lucia shrieked, "you're just about to be disowned!"

Joe lifted both his hands. "Okay, get him, tigress!"

She wasn't going to get anybody, and she knew it. She plunged toward the side of the pool, swimming desperately. She was a good swimmer. It was just that Ryan was better. In a second, he had her ankle.

She went down fast, toward the bottom of the pool; then he released her quickly. She still had plenty of air. And he wouldn't be expecting her to attempt revenge....

She reached the bottom of the pool, then used her
legs to propel herself hard toward the surface. She
came flying out and threw all her weight toward his
shoulders. She took him by surprise. He started sink-
ing, but he wasn't about to go alone.

He caught her by the wrist and dragged her back
down with him. They sank forever and ever together,
or so it seemed. Suddenly he dragged her against him,
then placed his foot on the bottom of the pool. He
pushed against it, and they both went shooting back
toward the surface.

Lucia could hear the children shrieking around
them, having the best of times. And Ryan was looking at her again, curiously, studying her. His gaze was
hot and piercing, and she shivered against him. She
returned his stare, and for the longest time she didn't
fight his hold. She felt their legs entwining in the cool
water, and she felt his hand move lightly against her
bare back.

"Lucia won, Lucia won!" Jimmy called out happily.

"She did not!" Giles protested indignantly. "Ryan
won, by a mile."

"Hey, who are you related to?" Theresa laugh-
ingly asked her son.

Ryan released Lucia and started swimming toward
the side of the pool. He hiked himself out, then turned
and waited. Lucia swam to the side.

He reached down to her, and she stared at his hand
for a long moment, then took it. Ryan lifted her easily from the water, setting her before him. He was still
holding her hand.

"I'm so glad they don't seem to be angry about the mixup in rooms anymore!" Aunt Faith whispered to Hope.

"You would think they'd known each other for ever!" Aunt Hope whispered in turn.

Ryan smiled very slowly, and Lucia knew that he had heard the whispering. He released her hand and turned away, picking up a towel from a lounge chair. He paused in front of Faith and Hope. "Thank you very much for the barbecue. It was delicious, and I had a wonderful time."

"Oh, you're very, very welcome!" Hope told him.

"Hey!" Joe called out. "What about goony golf? Aren't you going to come?"

Ryan paused, the towel cast carelessly around his neck. He looked at Lucia and smiled ruefully. "No. Thanks for the invitation, though. I've got, umm, a business meeting."

Joe nodded to him. *"Ciao."*

"Ciao," Ryan agreed. He looked thoughtfully at Lucia one more time, then turned and left the courtyard, heading for the elevators.

Chapter 4

The next day was relatively calm.

Or it would have been if Lucia hadn't spent the entire time worrying about the possibility that Ryan might show up.

Or maybe, she admitted to herself, she was worried about the possibility that he might *not* show up.

Lying in the sun with a huge straw hat covering her face, she reflected that goony golf had been a lot of fun. The women had easily thrashed the men—even though Frank and Bill and Leon and her uncles loved golf and had made reservations at almost every one of the numerous courses in the Myrtle Beach area. Sophie's score surpassed all the rest, but, on the whole, the women had a tendency to do better at getting the balls into the mouths of the dragons and other beasts that made up the course. Joe had spent the first half of the evening talking about the tremendous amount

of fun they were having and the second half swearing
that it was a dumb game and that he never wanted to
look at a golf ball again in his entire life. He'd had
them all laughing, and Lucia would have enjoyed
herself tremendously if...

If she had been able to forget Ryan Dandridge for
just ten minutes. Because of her, he hadn't come, and
she knew it. Or at least she'd thought she knew it. But
when they stopped off at the hotel for drinks and
snacks after the game, she had discovered how Ryan
had spent his evening: with a tall blonde. They had
been outside, dining on the terrace, and Lucia had
seen them through a plate-glass window. No one else
had noticed him, and she had tried very hard not to
watch him herself, but she had felt so eaten up inside
that she hadn't been able to resist. It wasn't that he
had been doing anything. The two of them had been
eating—king crab claws—and sipping wine—something white. They'd had coffee, but skipped desert.
And when they had finished their meal, Ryan had
helped the blonde out of her chair and into her wrap,
and Lucia had gritted her teeth, watching the way his
fingers grazed over the woman's shoulders. Ryan had
paid the bill, and then he and the blonde had walked
away along the beach.

She hadn't heard a thing anyone said after that.
And when they'd returned to the condominium, she
couldn't help wondering if the blonde was in Ryan's
apartment. She had stared up at his windows, but they
had been dark.

When she and Dina reached their apartment, she
mumbled some excuse about having left something in
the car. But she didn't run downstairs. Instead she ran

up. She wanted to knock on his door, but she'd realized that would be crazy, that it was his business what he did with his time, and who he did it with.

She fled back downstairs and was grateful to discover that Dina had already gone to bed. Lucia went into her own room, stripped and crawled into her nightshirt, then lay awake most of the night, consumed with jealousy.

Now it was late afternoon. Ryan hadn't appeared at all that day. Sophie and Theresa were dozing nearby, the twins and Mark were building a sand castle, and the Three Graces had the baby and Serena and Tracy upstairs with them while they prepared more food than anyone would ever eat.

Sophie sat up suddenly, stretching. She yawned, dug into the cooler for a diet soda and stretched again.

"Where has Dina gotten to today?" she asked, puzzled. "You know how she is about sun. She hates to miss a second of it."

Lucia rose on her elbows, tilted back her hat and shrugged. "I don't know. She wasn't around this morning when I woke up. Maybe she isn't as desperate for sun as you think. It's summer in Massachusetts, too, so she hasn't been freezing recently."

Sophie laughed. "That's right, we did have summer. It came on July seventeenth this year and lasted all day. Hey, it may be warm in September here, but back home, the nights are already cold. If I know Dina, she's out in the sun somewhere."

"She's a big girl. I'm sure she's all right," Theresa mumbled. "Besides, her mother is here. Aunt Faith can worry about her, and my mom and Hope can help.

I'm sure that's about all the worrying any grown woman could possibly need."

The three of them laughed, knowing that the Three Graces—and Patience, too—could worry about anything for days on end when they chose.

Lucia laughed in recognition; then her laughter slowly faded. She saw her Uncle Tony down the beach, and he wasn't alone. He was in his trunks, with a baseball cap over the shiny part of his bald pate. His hands were locked behind his back, he was looking out to sea, and he was listening to the man beside him: Gino Lopez.

"Lopez is back," Lucia said.

Theresa bolted up, looking at her father. "I'm going to find out what's going on," she said.

"Wait, I'll come with you." Lucia jumped up to follow her. Sophie, not about to be left, rose to join them, too.

They all went hurrying down the beach, Theresa in the lead. "Dad, hey, Dad!"

Tony looked up at them. Lucia thought that a quick look of dismay passed over his features, but then he smiled broadly. "Hi, there, girls, enjoying the day? It's delightful, huh? You all know Gino, right?"

They nodded. Gino gave them his big, reptilian smile, but Lucia didn't even try to smile in return. She just stared at him.

"Lucia, the little Lorenzo. Your parents aren't here, huh?" he said to her.

She shook her head.

"They're in Paris," Uncle Tony said. "Henry's thirtieth wedding anniversary present to Patience."

"Well, how nice. You tell your folks hello for me when you see them. We've missed them since they moved to Georgia."

Lucia smiled then. "Well, you've missed them for a while then. They moved before I was born."

"But they used to come for summers. Now—" He shrugged. "Now we don't get to see them very often. So you tell them hello for me, okay?"

"Sure."

"I guess I'll be going. See you, Tony. Oh—there's my son, Ron." He paused, narrowing his eyes and shading them with his hand. Lucia saw who he was pointing to, a tall, striking man with a dark tan, sandy hair and dark eyes. A sullen expression marred his good looks as he walked through the surf to the shore. Then he saw his father, and the group waiting for him, and a miraculous transformation seemed to take place. The sullen look left his face, and he smiled brightly, suddenly charming.

"Ron, come up here. You know Tony Chimino. This is his daughter, Theresa, and his nieces, Lucia and Sophie."

Lucia shook hands with Ron Lopez. She drew away as quickly as she could. He was very handsome, but she found it impossible to forget who his father was.

"Nice to meet you," she murmured. "I have to get back to the apartment. I'll see you all later."

She turned around and started back. A second later, Theresa and Sophie joined her.

"You should have seen him!" Theresa whispered.

"He was eating you up!" Sophie added.

"Who?"

"Ron Lopez. Actually, he isn't bad, Lucia. He's very good-looking, and Lopez is worth a fortune, you know."

"Yes, and remember how he got his money!" Lucia said. "I'm not interested."

She felt Theresa shrugging to Sophie behind her back. "Most of the men here are eating you up. With their eyes, I mean."

Lucia stopped walking. "What are you talking about?"

"You look good in a bathing suit, Lucia. Really good. You can take your pick of the men on the beach, you know."

"You could tell," Theresa continued, "with Ryan Dandridge last night."

Lucia started walking again, quickly. "You know, you're both sweethearts, but I'm really not looking for a man."

"Lucia, you're not getting any younger," Sophie warned her.

"And I'm not quite ready to keel over, either, thank you both very much!"

"He was really taken with you, I'm certain," Theresa said smugly. "Ryan Dandridge, I mean."

"It was almost as if you two had known each other before," Sophie teased.

"Really? How interesting."

"Now that is a man worth having," Theresa said firmly.

None of them realized that they had stopped right by the spot where the twins and Mark were building a sand castle. Giles stood up, grinning.

"Marry him, Cousin Lucia. If you do, we'll get to come here all the time."

"Giles!" his mother chastised him.

"I'll bear that in mind, Giles," Lucia said.

"He would be a great catch," Sophie said decidedly.

"A great catch?" Lucia threw her hands in the air. "What age are we living in? I'm an adult with a nice business and I support myself very well, thank you, and I don't need 'a great catch'!"

"The term has changed meaning, that's all," Theresa said lazily. "He's gorgeous, he's courteous and he's great with kids. And he's sexy as hell. And we're all human, and by a great catch, I mean a man with warmth and laughter and the right kind of personality. He's a great catch," she repeated firmly.

"I'm sure he is," Lucia murmured, dropping her eyes and searching desperately for a way to change the subject. She looked from Theresa to Sophie, certain that what she had to say would catch their interest. "What do you think is going on?" she asked in a low voice. "Last night Lopez was harassing Uncle Mario, and Uncle Paul jumped to his defense. Today it's your father."

"I don't like that man," Sophie said.

"Maybe he's just here on vacation," Theresa told them. "He's here with his son, after all."

"Maybe," Lucia said, shrugging. She didn't have any other answers. At least, not that she wanted to think about. "I'm going to shower."

"See you at cocktail hour," Theresa said.

"Cocktail hour?"

"We're going to have drinks and snacks at Frank's and Ellen's, and then move over to Charity's and Faith's for dinner. Sounds fun, just like a vacation."

Lucia laughed. "Just like a vacation."

They had reached the parking garage, and the sound of squealing tires caused them all to turn around.

Frank, Leon, Joe, Uncle Mario and Dina were all stuffed into a white Mercedes—and Ryan Dandridge was driving.

"The mystery of Dina is solved!" Theresa said.

"I didn't know she likes to golf," Sophie said.

"I don't think golf was the driving force, no pun intended," Theresa said.

Lucia didn't want to get stuck in the middle of this conversation and, most of all, she didn't want to see Ryan. She didn't want to see Dina laughing and putting her hands all over him.

Where was the blonde now? she wondered, then shrugged inwardly. But her fingers were trembling, and she really did need to get away. "I'm heading in. I really want a shower." She lifted her hand and waved to the returning golfers, then headed quickly for the elevator. She hit the button for her floor, and the elevator door closed behind her.

When the door opened at her floor, she found herself staring at Ryan, who was leaning casually against the wall, waiting for her.

"How did you get here?"

"I walked."

"You must have run like the wind."

"I walked quickly."

"Why?"

The doors started to close again, and he pulled her out of the elevator. She shrugged quickly away from his touch. "Oh, no, Mr. Dandridge. Hands off, remember?"

He scowled. "I was merely trying to get you out before the doors closed on you."

"You built this place. I know that an elevator door here would never close on me."

"Such faith. I do appreciate it, Lucia."

She ignored him and started walking toward her apartment, pulling out her key as she went. He followed her. He was in golf clothes: a white polo shirt; blue shorts; white socks and sneakers. He looked like an ad for a sporting-goods store. Bronzed, healthy, muscular, rugged and athletic.

The blonde had probably thought so, too.

To her distress, she fumbled with the key when she tried to open her door. He took the key from her fingers, and easily opened the door, pushing it inward. He made no attempt to come in, nor did she ask him, but when she tried to walk past him, he caught the door so she couldn't enter.

"What do you want?" she asked him.

"I want to know what you were doing outside my door last night."

"What?"

"Don't give me that wide-eyed innocent look. I heard you and I would have come out, except I wasn't dressed. By the time I put something on, you were gone."

Lucia pushed past him. "Not being dressed was a deterrent for you? Why? I imagine that half the population of Myrtle Beach and Garden City has seen you in the buff by now. Excuse me, will you?''

But he didn't excuse her.

The door slammed shut, and she jumped back, looking up at him. She hated being barefoot when he towered over her. She didn't much care for the angry pulse she saw beating in his throat, either.

''No, half of this place hasn't seen me in the buff, Ms. Lorenzo. Is *that* what this is all about?''

''I don't know what you're talking about.''

''Don't you?''

''No.''

''What were you doing up there?''

''I, er, I thought that I had lost an earring up there yesterday morning. Then I realized I hadn't.''

''So you were going to come and get it at midnight?''

''I realized how late it was and I left. Sorry I disturbed you.''

''Lucia, you're a liar, and a bad one. What did you want?''

''I didn't want anything,'' she said firmly. But her innocent pose wasn't going to work. He wasn't touching her, but he was almost on top of her. In a moment he was going to grab her arm and pull her close, leashing his anger so he didn't hurt her, but the tension would bubble and rise and cascade all around them, and then—

''Lucia, there you are. Ryan, are you coming in for a while?''

The moment was broken as Dina came hurrying off the elevator, smiling. She slipped her arm through

Ryan's. "It was hot out there today. Lucia, you look charbroiled, nearly as copper as a penny."

Ryan disentangled his arm, smiling at Dina. "I'm not coming in right now." He raised his eyes over her head, meeting Lucia's. "I think maybe I will come to the cocktail hour, though. See you then."

He turned and walked toward the elevator. Both women watched him go. Dina sighed. "Joe says he's carrying a torch."

"What?" Lucia demanded.

"Joe says he's just coming out of an affair that went sour on him. Who would leave a guy like that?"

Lucia didn't answer as she entered the condominium. Instead she said, "I *am* charbroiled. I'm going to hop straight into the shower."

Lucia went into the bathroom, eager to wash away the salt and the sand of the beach, and eager for the cold water that could momentarily take her mind off Ryan Dandridge.

Joe said that he was still carrying a torch....

Not for her. Besides, Ryan Dandridge didn't carry torches. He had a whole score of understudies in the wings at all times. Maybe it wasn't his fault. Maybe he just liked women, and they liked him in turn.

The bathroom door suddenly burst open. Lucia froze, panicked. Then she realized it was just Dina.

"Hey!" Dina called. "You've been in there forever! Thank goodness we're not paying for water here. I made you one of my specialities. It's a super-duper piña colada. It's on the sink when you come out."

"Thanks!"

"Sure thing."

A few moments later Lucia came out wrapped in a big towel. She sipped the drink and smiled—it *was* delicious.

Piña colada in hand, she wandered through her bedroom to the living room. She sat down, setting her drink on the coffee table, unwrapped the towel from her hair and started to dry it.

Then she heard Dina giggling from the balcony and realized that the doors were open, but it was too late. Dina stepped into the living room, already showered and dressed in a casual blue cocktail dress. Ryan followed her in. He, too, had already showered and changed. He was dressed in jeans and a tailored stone-washed shirt, and a casual soft fawn jacket lay over his arm. Both of them stopped and stared at Lucia, who was still clad in a towel.

She stared at them both in turn, muttered an expletive, then disappeared into her bedroom.

She leaned against her closed door, suddenly very frightened and unable to breathe. It had been one thing to bear the pain of leaving him when it was something private, something she had been able to endure from a great distance. But now he was everywhere she turned. With a blonde. With Dina. Her own damned cousin. It wasn't fair.

She pushed herself away from the door, tossing back her hair. She didn't care. She didn't care. She didn't care... let Dina suffer the heartache this time.

But she *did* care. She discovered that when she went to her closet. She chose a soft teal dress of swirling silk that was nearly backless, sheer stockings and four-inch heels. Then she swept her hair high off her neck in a French braid. When she was done, she stepped back.

The effect, she thought, was perfect. Mature, sophisticated. Pleased with herself, she picked up her evening bag and headed for the living room.

Then she paused for a moment, realizing that she was competing with her cousin. But I saw him first! she protested inwardly.

You saw him, but you couldn't handle the competition, and you ran away, she reminded herself.

She bit her lip. It didn't matter. She had to be cool and casual, and she had to hold her own.

They were still in the living room when she came out. Ryan was seated casually on the couch; Dina was across from him on the chair. He wasn't sipping one of Dina's piña coladas, though; he was drinking a beer.

They both stopped talking and stared at Lucia when she walked in and sat down across from Dina, picking up the drink she had left behind. She smiled at the two of them and sipped her drink.

"Lucia!" Dina said.

"What?"

"You look great. Doesn't she, Ryan?"

Lucia suddenly felt very ashamed of herself. Dina was always generous; and always played an honest game.

"Thanks, Dina," she said softly.

Ryan hadn't answered. He was staring at her, and she suddenly remembered the last time she had worn this dress. It had been the night before she had run away from him.

She swallowed the remainder of her drink and leaped to her feet. "Aren't we late? Shouldn't we be over at Frank's and Ellen's by now?"

Dina glanced at her watch. "Yes, I guess we should go. We were just waiting for you."

"That was nice," Lucia murmured. Ryan was still staring at her. "Well, let's go, okay?"

Ryan rose and helped Dina to her feet, and she slipped her arm through his. Lucia hurried out the door ahead of them.

It wasn't far to the other apartment, and Leon opened the door, ushering them in with a cheerful grin. "Just us middle-aged guys here. No parents, no children. How about that?"

"I'm all for it," Sophie said. "Dina, are you making piña coladas? I was waiting for you."

Lucia found a seat beside Joe, who grinned at her. Theresa took care of Ryan, bringing him a beer. There were crackers and cheese, and dips and chips, and the big glass window was open, letting in the sea breeze and revealing the crimson streaks on the horizon.

Lucia tried to ignore Ryan. He was sitting between Theresa and Sophie, who had him cornered, and were telling him family stories. Lucia was listening to Leon and Joe and Bill, as Joe told Bill about the little golf clubs Patience had once bought for Frank, and how Frank had opened a huge gash in Joe's head with one.

"On purpose?"

"Heck, no. Frank was five and I was three. But boy, did Patience feel bad."

"Patience," Ryan said thoughtfully, and Lucia looked over at him. He was watching them, smiling wryly. "That's not an Italian name, is it?"

Joe grinned. "Nope. Gramps was in love with Massachusetts. He liked the stories about the May-flower and the pilgrims and all. That's why he had

Faith, Hope and Charity—and Patience.'' Joe affec-
tionately tweaked Lucia's cheek. "Then our parents
chose whatever names they wanted.''

"Piña coladas, the Dina Donatello special,'' Dina
announced, coming in from the kitchen. She stopped
in front of Lucia first. "Take one.''

Lucia hesitated. She was already feeling the effects
of the first.

"Lucia, hurry up, before I drop them!''

She took a drink, then realized that Joe was staring
at her strangely. She stared back, but he only smiled.
Meanwhile, Dina was over by Ryan, laughing about
something.

She sipped her drink. She needed it.

In another few minutes they moved next door for
dinner.

Faith, Hope and Charity were beaming, and Lucia
thought that, even for her aunts, they had outdone
themselves. The sisters had spent the day with Charity's pasta machine, so the cappelletti and ravioli were
fresh. Faith had made her special eggplant and meatballs, Charity had done sausage and peppers, and
there was even a big bowl of "robbies," or ribbinis, an
Italian vegetable similar to mustard greens. They were
Joe's favorite, so he immediately made a fuss over
them, and all the sisters were happy.

The scene was mass confusion; there were just too
many people in the small apartment and spilling out
onto the balcony. Lucia wound up on a lounge chair
with Theresa; Ryan was right across from them. The
baby was crawling across the floor, and it seemed that
children were everywhere. Lucia dared to glance at
Ryan, wondering what he was thinking of the family,

of all this domesticity. Then she wondered just how much she really knew about him.

Dina came by and perched on the edge of his chair, whispering to him, and he laughed easily. The blonde last night; Dina today. She knew enough about him, Lucia decided firmly. But it still hurt. It hurt so badly that she swallowed down several big gulps of her drink, enjoying the nice soft blur of emotion it brought her. It was one thing to know that he wasn't good for her. It was another to try to fall out of love with him.

"More meatballs?" Aunt Faith said.

"No, thanks," Frank called back.

"Oh, dear. Were they all right?"

Frank stood up and hugged her. "They were delicious, Aunt Faith. Really delicious."

"Then have another. There are plenty left."

"Ma!" Joe piped up, laughing. "We can't win, you know. We can't possibly win. If there are any meatballs left, that means that we didn't like them. If we eat them all, you worry that you didn't make enough."

"They were delicious, Mrs. Donatello. Really delicious," Ryan told her, smiling. "The best I've ever had."

Five minutes later, whether he wanted it or not, Ryan was sitting there with another plate of meatballs. Dina had gone for more drinks, and Theresa had left to fix a plate for Tracy.

Except for the others chatting in the background, Ryan and Lucia were alone. She thought about rising, about finding something to do. But the two piña coladas had made her lethargic, and she didn't seem to have the strength.

Ryan looked at his plate, then happened to meet Lucia's eyes when he looked up. He grinned sheepishly. "What do I do now?"

"Eat your meatballs," she told him gravely.

"Have one?"

She shrugged. She probably should help rescue him. "All right. One. You'll have to pawn the others off elsewhere."

"What a terrible thing· to say about your aunt's meatballs."

"I love my aunt's meatballs. I just know enough to keep my mouth shut when I've already eaten my fill."

"Come here."

He'd skewered a meatball, cut it in half and lifted the fork. He intended to put it into her mouth. She wasn't sure why it seemed like such an intimate gesture—any one of her cousins might have done the same. But this was . . . different.

Still, to her own surprise, she obeyed him. She moved forward and took the morsel from his fork; his eyes were on her mouth all the while. She felt a flash of heat and she quickly withdrew, telling herself that it was impossible to make something erotic out of a meatball.

But it wasn't impossible at all. Ryan had done it.

"How's it going?" Dina was back. She sat on the edge of Ryan's chair again. "Need some help with those things?" She picked up the fork and finished off one of the meatballs. "Hey, Joe, come take one of these things for Ryan. If everybody eats at least half a meatball, we can take care of them all. Ryan will be saved, and Mom will be happy."

Joe, Leon and Frank each took a meatball, and Ryan was indeed rescued. Dina was laughing again, and leaning close to Ryan. Lucia felt as if she were choking. There had to be something she could do. She had to escape.

"Leon?" she asked.

"Yeah?"

"Let's go do dishes."

"I've got a better idea. Let's head for a nightclub."

"A nightclub?"

"Someplace with a good band and dancing."

"Help me do some of the dishes first. Then I'm with you."

"Deal. Although they always rewash dishes when I do them, you know."

Lucia laughed. "You can dry." She hopped up with Leon, feeling as if Ryan's eyes were following her. She felt the heat of his gaze all the way down the length of her spine.

But when she reached the kitchen she turned around and saw that he wasn't watching her at all. He was leaning close to Dina, and he was laughing again.

In the end, neither she nor Leon had to wash or dry. For one thing, the condominiums all came with dishwashers. For another, Aunt Faith shooed them away. "Go on, now. You young folks go on out and have a good time."

"I'd have a better time if you'd let me do something first," Lucia insisted.

"Don't worry about it," Aunt Faith said firmly. "Now go on."

"Only if we get to take you all out later, in return," Lucia insisted.

"Fine. That will be very sweet. Now go."

Frank and Ellen caught up with them before they reached the elevator. "Where are you off to?" Ellen demanded.

Leon named the nightclub in one of the big hotels on the beach. Frank said to hold the elevator, then ran back to invite Theresa and Bill to come along.

Lucia felt a little warning prickle of unease, but she shook it off. Ryan wouldn't appear. And if he did, he would have Dina on his arm. One woman per night, she thought wryly, should be enough for him.

Her fears were silly, she assured herself. Ryan and Dina weren't coming with them, and Bill and Theresa would most probably be coming later. She could—and would!—go out and gave a good time!

The nightclub was packed. The band played top-forty music and golden oldies, along with an occasional big-band number for the older members of their audience. It was a cute place, decorated like a mariner's shanty with pieces of boats and figureheads and ship's wheels hung on the knotty-pine walls. The rear was all glass windows, revealing the balcony and the steps that led down to the beach.

They found a table inside and ordered their drinks; then Leon pulled Lucia onto the dance floor. "Don't look now," he said. "Don't look now, but..."

The hairs at her nape began to rise. Had Ryan followed them? Or worse! It could be Gino Lopez, stalking one of them.

"What!" she nearly shrieked.

"There is the most gorgeous blonde I have ever seen in my entire life just over there. And she's with girls. I mean, she doesn't seem to be on a date. Let's dance that way."

"A blonde?"

"Yeah, a blonde."

"Leon, I could throw you off the balcony. You scared me to death."

"How?"

"Never mind. And what is this male obsession with blondes? What's the matter with dark hair?"

"Nothing." He kissed her forehead. "Yours is just gorgeous. It's just that you're my cousin, and she isn't. Come on, would you, dance this way?"

Lucia obligingly danced toward the table with the beautiful blonde. When they reached the edge of the floor, they stopped dancing. Leon managed to swirl her into a chair right next to his target. He smiled at the blonde, who cast an uneasy gaze Lucia's way. "Talk to them!" Leon whispered to her. "Tell her in some subtle way that you're my cousin."

Lucia smiled sweetly. "He's my cousin!" she called over the music.

"Not like that!" Leon protested. "I said subtle."

Lucia grinned, then asked the blonde if she was on vacation and if she was having a good time. The other woman's name turned out to be Lucy, and she seemed very sweet. She also seemed to like the way Leon looked. Lucia was glad, since she thought Leon was pretty special.

"He's really your cousin?" Lucy asked her.

"Really. We're here for a family reunion. I have cousins everywhere, I think." She smiled and excused herself. Leon, in seventh heaven, slid into a chair at the table with Lucy and her two friends.

Lucia went back to her own table. Frank and Ellen
were on the dance floor, while Bill and Theresa had yet
to arrive.

The drinks had come while she was dancing with
Leon. She idly played with her straw, then took a sip.
The drink was strong, but not as strong, Lucia realized, as those Dina had made. She would have to quit
after this one. She wasn't driving, but the world was
beginning to look a little too fuzzy anyway.

"Hi."

She started. A strange man was standing over the
table, smiling at her.

"My name is Michael Greene. I'm a friend of
Lucy's, and I understand that the gentleman over
there is not your date, but your cousin. Would you
consider a dance?"

It was a come-on, but she was in a nightclub, and
people did come to such places to dance. And Michael Greene seemed to be okay. He was tall and thin
and had nice amber eyes, and he was attractively
dressed in a casual tan jacket and dark trousers. She
didn't really want to dance, though. "No, thanks,"
she said, smiling.

"Just one dance?"

"No, I don't think—"

Just then she saw that Theresa and Bill had made it
at last. They were weaving their way through the
crowd—and they were not alone. Dina and Ryan had
come with them.

Dina immediately dragged Ryan out to the floor. It
was a slow dance, and Lucia saw that her cousin was
crushed to Ryan's chest.

Lucia made a sudden decision. "I'd love to dance." She gave Michael Greene a dazzling smile. He responded with pleasure, sweeping her into his arms and onto the floor.

Lucia had no idea what Michael Greene said to her after that, but it didn't matter. She laughed and stared up at him with starry eyes, moving her fingers idly over his shoulders as she fluidly followed his lead. He danced well, and she knew they made a good couple. If anyone was looking, that was.

Jealousy. It was going to get her into a lot of trouble.

The band played on, the tempo changing. Lucia still wasn't terribly sure what Michael Greene was talking about, but she kept nodding and smiling and laughing away. She was breathless, and the music was loud, and the lights were spinning all around her.

"Want to take a break?" He spoke loudly enough that his words managed to penetrate her brain.

"What?" she yelled back.

"Take a break! It's hot in here. Want to take a walk out on the balcony?"

She looked around. She didn't see Dina or Ryan, or even Bill and Theresa or Frank and Ellen. She suddenly felt tired, and it was very hot.

"Fine, that would be nice."

Michael Greene led her through the crowd, and a wave of cool air hit them as soon as he opened the door. Lucia stepped out to the deck and walked over to the rail. The moon was up. It was high and almost full, really beautiful. It was a great night for lovers. If only she could be with the man she loved.

"Nice night," Michael said. "There's a little bit of beach left. Let's walk."

He set his hand casually on her shoulder and guided her toward the stairs. "See, just a strip. Sometimes the tide is so high that the beach disappears completely."

"Does it?"

They walked down to the sand. The night was dark once they were away from the bright lights of the club. Lucia walked for a while, enjoying the air, hearing the soothing rhythm of the surf. If they kept walking, they would eventually reach the condos.

Lucia realized that her shoes were filling with sand, so she paused to take them off. "I'm not sure this is such a great idea." She laughed, wiggling her toes to get rid of the sand that had sifted through her stockings.

"Take your stockings off."

There was something about his tone that she didn't like. She looked up at him. "I'm all right."

"Let's go. You know, you have a fabulous smile." He was holding her elbow, and for a thin man, he had a good, strong grasp. He spoke quietly, but she liked his tone even less.

"Let's go back," she said flatly.

But he didn't intend to go back. He swung her around to face him, staring down at her.

"You have the nicest, sexiest smile and the nicest eyes. I could read things in those eyes, in the way you were looking at me, the way you flirted and laughed. I kept asking you if you were ready, and you just kept nodding."

"What?" She felt ill. Her knees were trembling, and she was desperate to remember anything he might have said, anything at all.

"I asked you if you were in the mood. And you flashed that smile at me, and I felt ready, too, really ready. Don't play hard to get now. It's too late, gorgeous. You asked for it. You asked for it pretty and sweet."

"What?"

The strangled word had barely left her lips before his mouth descended hard on hers. He wrenched her against him, then placed his free hand flat on her breast.

Gasping and struggling with rage, Lucia tried to free herself, but he was very strong, and she couldn't get away. She managed to dislodge his hand, but he only set it on her thigh, lifting the hem of her dress.

She pulled her lips free at last. "Stop it!"

"Sure, sweetheart." He laughed and picked her up, and in a moment he was falling on top of her in the sand. For the first time she realized that Michael Greene had been drinking heavily, and that she just might be in real trouble.

"Listen, you overgrown delinquent, you stop it this instant!" His hands were all over her, and she couldn't move because of his weight. He kept smiling, but it was an alcohol-induced smile, Lucia realized. "Stop it!" she shouted again.

"Hold still now, honey, and keep that sparkle in your eyes for me, huh? It will be worth your while," he said as he began to unbutton his shirt.

"No!"

She gritted her teeth, ready for battle, but there was no one to fight. A hand had landed on Michael Greene's shoulder, and suddenly he was gone; then she saw him land on the sand about ten feet away.

Lucia straightened her skirt and scrambled away.

Ryan was there, just a foot in front of her, staring with distaste from her to Michael Greene.

"Hey!" Michael Greene protested. "This is my date. You go back and get your own."

"She isn't your date. And she said no."

"She meant yes."

Ryan walked over and stared down at Michael where he lay in the sand. "Listen, I sympathize."

"You what?" Lucia flared.

He ignored her and kept talking to Michael. "From the way she was looking at you in there, you had every reason to think what you did, but I did very distinctly hear her say, 'no,' and it sounded plenty clear to me."

"So who are you, her brother?" Michael demanded belligerently.

Ryan smiled coldly. "A friend of the family. Lucia, get up."

"Ryan, don't you—"

"Lucia, get up!"

She didn't feel like arguing with him. In fact, she felt rather ashamed of herself. She stood up quickly, finding her shoes where they lay in the sand.

"Hey, you can't just take off with her!" Michael protested. He staggered to his feet, staring at Ryan.

"I can, and I intend to."

"No, man, hey..." He walked a few feet toward Ryan, smiled and raised his fists. Then he started swinging.

Ryan ducked once, then hit Michael with an upper-cut to the jaw. Michael went right down. He rubbed his jaw and stared sullenly at Ryan.

"Sorry," Ryan said. "I didn't want to do that. I suggest you sober up a bit before going back. And as for you..." He turned to Lucia. His eyes looked as cold and hard as blue diamonds. He grabbed her hand, and his hold was merciless. "Let's go. Now."

He started toward the steps, jerking her along in his wake. Suddenly he stopped, and she crashed into his back. "Say good night to Michael."

She turned around. "Good night, Michael."

She felt a tremendous jerk on her hand, and she was pulled more than led up the stairway to the lounge.

But they didn't go back to the table, and they didn't stop to talk to any of her relatives. Instead Ryan led her angrily right through the crowd and out to the front, where his white Mercedes was waiting.

Lucia, both frightened and angered by his temper, balked. "Ryan, thank you. You got me out of a difficult situation—"

"Attempted rape is a difficult situation to you? I'll remember that. Now get in the car. You're drunk, and you're going home."

She bit her lip. "Ryan, I'm not drunk, and you're not my brother. You're not even one of my cous—"

"Get in the car."

"I can go home with Leon."

"Get in the car!" He moved toward her menacingly. "Or I'll get you into it myself, Ms. Lorenzo!"

"You would not. You're not supposed to touch me!"

He took another step toward her, and she let out a gasp and leaped into the passenger seat. Without another word, he climbed in beside her and revved the car's engine.

Chapter 5

It wasn't far from the hotel to the condominium, and Lucia wished it were much, much farther.

Ryan didn't say a word during the drive, and neither did she. He brought the car to a halt in his parking spot, then sat in the driver's seat, his fingers wound tightly around the steering wheel.

Lucia sat still for a moment herself. Then she reached for the door handle. "Thank you very much for the ride...and the help. I appreciate it very much." She started to open the car door, but he leaned over her and closed it with a sharp, meaningful slam. His cologne filled her senses, and the fabric of his soft jacket brushed her flesh, awakening her nerve endings.

"Ryan—"

"What in hell did you think you were doing?"

"I went out dancing!" Lucia flared angrily. "What's the matter with that?"

She folded her hands tightly in her lap and stared out the window. She didn't want to think about the appeal of his scent, or the jut of his chin and the flash in his eyes. She didn't want to think about the car, with its soft maroon leather interior. They had gone too many places in that car. And they had come home from too many places in it, too. Home, to the rustic old Cape Cod house near Newport, where he had enclosed the porch in glass and set up a Jacuzzi, overlooking the snows of winter.

His fingers remained wound around the steering wheel, but he twisted to stare at her with amazement and fury. "You just can't admit when you're wrong, can you, Lucia?"

"When I'm wrong! I went dancing—"

"And you smiled at him like a two-bit hooker."

"A two-bit hooker!" Lucia flared. She reached for the door handle again, but he caught her wrist before she could open it. Her eyes met his, and she narrowed them fiercely. "You mean what he did was all right because I was flirting?"

"Listen, Lucia, I didn't say it was all right. He was in the wrong, okay? He was definitely in the wrong. But you did get yourself into the situation. And you *were* acting just like a little tease."

Her heart beating frantically, she looked at her wrist, then at Ryan. "Is the lecture over?"

"Maybe," he snapped.

She snatched her wrist away, rubbing it. "What about you, Mr. Dandridge? What if your cheap little blonde had decided to get rough with you? Of course, you probably wanted her to get carried away. You—"

"What cheap little blonde?"

Lucia stiffened. "I don't know. Whatever blonde you last happened to be out with. You're always out with someone."

"There's a difference," he said.

"Oh?"

"I know what I'm doing. You don't."

"You know, Ryan, I did manage to stumble through life before I met you."

"So you did. Stumble, that is."

Before she realized what was happening, he opened his door and came around to hers. He pulled it open and reached to help her out. She wanted to ignore him, but Ryan never let himself be ignored. He took her hand and pulled her out of the car.

She wasn't sure what happened next. She didn't know if the piña coladas or the sun or the heat, or maybe even Ryan himself, had suddenly gotten to her. She tried to stand on her own two feet, but she swayed, nearly falling.

"Lucia, what's wrong?"

His arms swept around her, and she heard the concern in his voice. It was nice. It was very nice. She smiled weakly. "I don't know...."

"I do." The concern was gone. "You're smashed. Plain old smashed. You went out and got smashed and asked for trouble and you got it." He swept her off the ground into his arms, intending to carry her. His teeth were clenched tightly together.

He was right, in a way, but she wasn't going to admit it. "Ryan, I am not drunk. And I can walk. Put me down."

"You can't walk. You'll fall again."

"You're not supposed to be touching me."

"It's the only way I can figure out to carry you, Ms. Lorenzo."

"But I don't need to be carried."

"You do."

He jabbed his finger against the elevator button. There was a soft whirring sound, and when the elevator appeared, he stepped into it.

"You really should put me down," she told him. "What if one of my aunts comes out?"

"I'll tell her that I'm putting a lush to bed."

"I am not a lush."

"Lay off the piña coladas, then. Your cousin puts enough booze in them to pickle you for life."

She didn't know why, but she smiled, and her fingers curled around his neck. It was insane to get close to him again. Absolutely insane. But at the moment she didn't care. She felt serene, completely peaceful and glad to be carried in his arms. "Where is my cousin? Weren't you her escort?"

"Nope. We didn't even come in the same car."

"No?"

"Theresa drove with me, and Bill went with Dina. I thought I might want to leave early."

"Oh?"

"Yes," he said flatly.

The elevator reached the second floor, and he started walking down the hallway. "Where's your key?"

"In my pocket." No sooner had she found it than he took it from her and unlocked the door. She kept watching his face as she spoke. "Dina is a stunning woman."

"Yes, she is."

"She's fun, and she's a real sweetheart."

"Yes, I think so."

He pushed the door open with his foot and carried her in, flicking the hallway switch and turning on the light along the way. Then he closed the door and started unerringly for her bedroom.

His bedroom. The room where they had unknowingly slept together that first night.

He carried her in and laid her on the bed, then slipped her shoes off and set them on the floor. Lucia watched him, wondering what would happen next.

He came back to her and leaned over her, bracing his weight on his palms on either side of her head. He smiled. "She's beautiful, she's bright and she's charming. But she doesn't compare with you, Lucia."

He lowered his head and caught her lips with his own. The touch was light and tender and painfully sweet. Then his mouth pressed more fully against hers, the pressure of his tongue parting her teeth. Slowly, sensually, he licked her inner lip, and she parted her mouth farther, reaching up for him. She trailed her fingers through his hair and over his nape. She brushed the tips of them over his cheek, and she felt his hands brush like velvet over her shoulders and caress the fullness of her breast.

Then he broke away from her, but his face remained just inches away from hers, and his hand still rested intimately on her breast. "Want to know something else about Dina?"

"What?" she whispered, confused, still tasting the sweet fire of his kiss.

"She's home."

"She's what?"

"Listen. She's home. She just came in."

"Oh!" Dismayed, Lucia bolted up. Ryan pressed a finger against her lips. "It's all right." He smiled. "See you tomorrow, Lucia."

He turned around and left her, closing her bedroom door. She heard Dina talking to him in the hallway. "Ryan! What's wrong? Is Lucia all right? I heard that you left with her in a bit of a whirl."

"She's fine. She met with a rather insistent guy on the beach and I rescued her, that's all. I think she twisted her ankle a bit, so I helped her up here."

"Oh. Maybe I should check on her."

"I think she's almost asleep. She's fine, really."

"Oh. Oh, well. Can I make you some coffee or something?"

"Not a thing, thanks."

Lucia heard a pause, then a soft, curious sound. Ryan had kissed Dina on the forehead, or the cheek— or so Lucia hoped.

"Good night, Dina."

"See you tomorrow."

"Sure."

The outer door opened and closed. Smiling, Lucia closed her eyes and fell almost instantly asleep.

Lucia awoke very early, still in her cocktail dress. She rose and showered and put on her blue bikini, her favorite suit. Then she grabbed her glasses and her hat, determined to head right out to the beach and lie in the sun.

Dina was already up, and coffee was on. "Want a cup?" her cousin offered.

"Sure!"

Dina was dressed for the water, too. Her suit was a white maillot, and it looked gorgeous on her. Lucia remembered Ryan's words of the night before, and she smiled even as she sipped her coffee. She could have no future with him. She was being a fool. Still, it was nice to remember his words, and to cherish them.

"I hear you had some trouble last night," Dina said.

Lucia shrugged. "A bit."

"Men! You dance with them, and they think they own you."

Lucia laughed. "Well, it all worked out all right. You coming down to the beach?"

"Yes. You ready? Or do you want to eat something first?"

"No, the coffee was great. Let's wait a while, and then we can walk along to one of the little restaurants and grab something."

"Sounds good."

Lucia packed a rattan bag with a few dollars, their towels and sunscreen. They left the room together, and Dina locked the door. They had started toward the elevators when Lucia paused, certain that she'd heard fast, angry voices.

"Dina, wait."

She had heard voices, coming from above them. She moved over to the railing and tried to look up, but the morning sun dazzled her eyes, and she had to blink against it.

"Lucia!" Dina whispered.

"Shh!" Whatever was going on wasn't any of her business, but she was worried, though she didn't know why.

She stepped back suddenly. She had glimpsed the pair who were arguing. It was Lopez. Lopez was back, and he was arguing with her cousin Frank.

What was it? What was going on? Why did the uninvited loan shark keep having heated discussions with members of her family?

"Who is it?" Dina demanded.

"Frank."

"And?"

Lucia looked at her uneasily. "Lopez."

Dina waved a hand. "I wouldn't worry. Frank probably just wants him to stay away from his father and get out of here. Frank is as pure as the driven snow. You know that."

Lucia cast her a dry glance. "We're all as pure as the driven snow."

Dina chuckled. "Well...that depends."

"Dina!"

"All right, all right. We're all as pure as the driven snow. But the man is a loan shark, and Lucia you know as well as I do that half of Boston has been in debt to him at one time or another. Don't worry about it. He's here on vacation with his son. No problem. Okay?"

Lucia hesitated for a minute, then shrugged. "Okay. I'm not worried. I mean, a rotten loan shark seems to be following us around, but I won't worry."

"Good. Let's get down to the beach."

It was going to be another beautiful day. There wasn't a single cloud in the sky, which was already a glorious blue. Lucia lay down beside Dina and felt the sun caress her cheeks and thighs; she closed her eyes, and her mind drifted to Ryan.

She was such a fool. She couldn't change things. Dina said that a man could be caught, but she didn't want to *catch* a man. She wanted him to want the same commitment she did. She wanted him to be in love with her as deeply as she was with him.

There was no problem just being with Ryan on a temporary basis. She rolled over, pressing her cheek against the hot sand. It was so easy to be with him. But it would hurt her all over again. When she walked away again, her heart would be in tatters. She needed to be polite and friendly—and to stay away from him. She should have left, no matter how good the reunion.

Dina tapped her on the shoulder. "It's ten, and I'm starving. Let's get something to eat."

Lucia agreed. They walked down the beach, found an open restaurant and ordered toast and eggs. Theresa and Bill, along with the kids, found them there.

"A football game. That's what we need. A good game of touch football in the sand. How does that sound?"

"Sandy," his wife replied dryly.

"You're going to love it. Trust me."

Theresa rolled her eyes. "That's what he said about childbirth."

But by the time they finished breakfast more of the family had gathered on the beach, and Joe and Leon jumped right in on the idea. Two teams were quickly formed. Joe was one captain; Bill was the other. Lucia quickly found herself playing with Joe and Leon, while Bill took his wife and Frank. Ellen and Theresa wound up on Joe's team, along with Uncle Mario, and Bryce and Katie went with Bill. The twins opted to play with their father, so Mark and Serena played with Bill. Tracy and Valerie were left on a blanket with Sophie, who absolutely refused to join in. "Someone has to watch the small fry," she insisted.

"Hey, I'll do it," Lucia volunteered, but Sophie had made up her mind, and Joe told Lucia she wasn't going to get out of the game that easily.

By the end of the first play, Joe's team had already made a touchdown. Lucia had gotten to carry the ball all the way past the goal line marked by a palm tree and a beach blanket.

"That's unfair!" Bill said. "You've got more people. Mario's a team all by himself."

"Hey. Life is unfair, right?" Joe teased back.

But Bill was suddenly smiling. "Look who's coming. And he's going to be on my team."

Lucia spun around. Ryan was there.

Warmth sizzled through her, and she lowered her eyes, thinking that just seeing him was bad for her. She had to get a grip on her emotions.

He was wearing his black bathing trunks, and a St. Christopher's medal gleamed from the thick mat of dark hair on his chest. He had on a pair of sunglasses, so she couldn't see his eyes, but she realized that he hadn't been coming their way.

Maybe he'd been having second thoughts, too. He must have been trying to avoid the family, but there was no avoiding Bill when he was determined.

"Ryan. Ryan! Hey!" He waved his arm frantically. "We need you. We're getting creamed by a bunch of girls over here!"

"Hey, I resent that," Dina said. But she, too, raised her voice. "Ryan, come on, please, lend a hand over here!"

Lucia saw Ryan hesitate. Then he turned her way.

"Ryan, come on!" Bill pleaded.

Ryan shrugged to Lucia, as if he had no control over the situation, which was true. He trotted toward Bill, and a cheer went up from the family.

Lucia looked down the beach, in the direction where he had been headed. There was a blonde in a lounge chair down there. A beautiful blonde. It had to be the same woman as the other night, though she was wearing a hat over her face, so Lucia couldn't be certain of anything except that she felt ill.

Bill's team received the ball. Ryan caught it and tore down the beach. Neither Lucia nor anyone on her team could come close to him, and the score was quickly tied.

Mark managed to make a touchdown for Lucia's team next, though she was certain Ryan had been careful not to catch him.

Bill made a touchdown all on his own the next time, so of course Joe had to equal him. Then it was Dina's turn to run with the ball, and her brother wasn't about to let her succeed. Joe clobbered her about five feet before the goal line.

"Hey!" Dina protested. "This is touch football."

"Yeah, but you didn't stop."

"Oh, I was supposed to stop?"

Laughing, Lucia helped Dina up. She tried to catch Ryan's eyes, but he was still wearing his dark glasses, and she couldn't read a thing from his expression.

"We're one ahead!" Joe said jubilantly. "Now let's keep the lead. Whoever catches the ball, just run like hell. No sneak plays, just run!"

Ryan was about to kick. Lucia watched as Bill held the ball and Ryan came racing for it, sending it sailing.

Lucia looked up, watching it rise in a high arc against the shimmering blue sky. It began to come down, falling straight toward her.

She reached out and gasped as the pigskin plummeted into her waiting hold, nearly knocking the breath from her. "Run, Lucia, run!" Joe screamed, jumping up and down with his words.

She ran.

She dodged Dina easily, and she even managed to slip by the twins, because Joe and Uncle Mario ran great interference. She had a clear shot at the goal line. Hugging the ball tightly, she sprinted with all her energy toward it.

Then she felt arms around her waist, and suddenly she was lying flat on the ground, spitting out sand. She gasped for breath and twisted, opening her eyes—and stared into Ryan's eyes.

His sunglasses had fallen off, and his eyes were as blue as the sky. He didn't smile; he didn't even seem to realize that he was lying half over her. He just stared down at her, and the sun began to seem hotter, the breeze lighter, as the heat of the day shimmered around them. A tremor ran through him, and for a moment the raw longing inside him was so visible that it brought anguish to her soul. She wondered instantly if her eyes were so naked, so pained.

Then the look was gone, washed away, as if it had been taken by the surf. Ryan leaped to his feet and reached down, brooking no resistance as he helped her to hers. He turned around and waved to Bill. "Hey! I've got to get into town. Sorry to be a quitter. See you all later."

As quickly as that he left. Lucia watched as he trotted away.

The game was over for her, too. It seemed that the sun had ceased to shine, and the breeze to stir. She waved to Joe. "I'll get the kids and make Sophie come out here for a while!"

Later on they all decided to try a new smorgasbord in town for dinner. Lucia was quiet, and Joe glanced at her curiously. "You are coming, aren't you, Lucia?"

"No, uh, I think I'm going to stick around tonight and get some sleep, okay?" Actually, she planned to take some time to think about just what was happening to her. Besides, what if they invited Ryan along? She didn't think she could stand it.

"No, Lucia, come on!" Dina protested.

But Lucia was firm. She went down to the beach with her cousins later in the afternoon for drinks and snacks, but she remained adamant about dinner. When they decided to go in and change, she lay back and waved.

"You're going to turn into a raisin," Dina warned her.

"I have great olive skin and tons of sun block," Lucia assured her. She sat up. "Look, I'm happy. I want to be alone tonight. I'm tired. Honest. I'll be back with the flow by tomorrow, I promise."

"Okay, kid. See you in the a.m."

"Right."

She set her hat over her face and drifted into a light doze. She could still hear children playing on the beach, and the sound of the surf.

"Lucia."

She looked up and smiled. Dina was back. She was in a soft gray pantsuit and looked terrific. Lucia whistled at her.

"Thanks.' Dina grinned. "Too bad you aren't an eligible guy. I came down to see if you want to change your mind and come."

Lucia shook her head. "No, but thanks."

"Party poopers."

"Plural?" Lucia quizzed her.

"Yeah, we couldn't talk Ryan into going out tonight, either. Joe went up to ask him to come with the group, but he said he couldn't. I wonder why."

"Maybe he has another date."

"I don't think so. I think he wanted to come, but he refused for some reason. Oh, who knows."

"Did he, er, know that I wasn't coming?"

"We didn't say anything. Why?" Dina demanded curiously.

"No reason, just curious," Lucia said quickly. She hesitated, wondering if she could change quickly and join them. But Dina was already on her way, tiptoeing over the sand and waving goodbye. "I see Joe at the car. I'm going to get over there before he starts with one of his fits. Boy, do I feel sorry for the girl he finally marries.''

Lucia smiled and waved in turn. ''Have a good time.''

''We'll miss you.''

''Good. You're supposed to!''

Lucia watched until Dina was in the car and the whole group of them had driven away. Then she lay back in the sand and stared up at the sky. This was stupid. She should have gone with them.

She lay there for a while, but she was too restless to enjoy the soft breeze of early evening. After a while she stood and started walking down the beach. The surf curled over her toes, and the sand squeezed between them. Tiny crabs hurried for cover. It was growing late. All the mothers were bringing their little ones in for dinner. The beach belonged to her now, and to a few teenagers and scattered lovers, but even as she walked, the water crawled higher up the sand, which, more and more was hers and hers alone.

There was a break in the seawall by a set of wooden stairs. Lucia wandered over and sat on the wall, watching the night come in. The sunset was so beautiful as it fell over the Atlantic. A rainbow of soft colors burst forth, and the water shimmered beneath a boundless blanket of gold and magenta.

It was a time not to be alone, she thought. The view was one that should be shared by lovers.

She drew her knees up beneath her and hugged her arms around them. If only there was no such thing as the future. If only reality was the illusion, and fantasy was the truth.

I'm in love with him again, she thought, feeling the soft air of the night wash over her. No…she had never fallen out of love with him. But she had known from the very beginning that Ryan Dandridge had no desire for a lasting commitment. He had told her as much, honestly, openly.

She smiled slightly, remembering how adamant she had been in return. She, too, had been wary of commitment of any kind and had seriously doubted that she would ever marry again. She had been married once, for all of six weeks. It had been after high school and before college, a sheer disaster from start to finish. She had been determined, infatuated with the idea of being in love. His name had been Tim Dickerson, and he had been captain of the high-school football team. Her friends had all warned her that he was the love 'em and leave 'em type, but Lucia had assured them that he wouldn't leave her—and he hadn't. They had eloped, and within a week they had both regretted the action with all their hearts. Tim wanted a temptress in bed, but he himself hadn't had the sensitivity of a chimp. In the miserable little apartment that they had rented, he had wanted a mother and a maid. He didn't want to let his wife out of the apartment, except to go to work. He even resented it when she went to visit her family.

Lucia had still believed in her own future, and she hadn't been about to scrub floors and work nine to six at the fast-food shack to put Tim through college. When she tried to explain that to him, he had slapped her, and that had been the end of her fantasy. She had packed her bags the second he left the house and gone home. And though it had been a humiliating experience, it had also been the best move she had ever made. Her mother had let her cry, and her father had never once said, "I told you so." They had suggested that she get an annulment instead of a divorce, and to please them, she had gone through the painful process. It had taken her two years. And long after those two years had passed, she had avoided men like the bubonic plague.

It had been easy to assure Ryan Dandridge that she had no interest in marriage whatsoever. Except that it had slowly become a lie. Or maybe not so slowly. It was as if from the moment they met she had known that he was the right man for her. And no matter how much she had tried to deny it, even to herself, things hadn't changed. She'd loved him then, and she loved him now.

He hadn't wanted commitment . . . and neither had she. But they had barely met and begun dating before her thoughts were only of him. She'd known him only two weeks when they first made love, and two weeks later they were living together. She had forgotten all about going home to Atlanta, to her family, work or friends. It had been so easy to stay with him. . . .

Until, of course, she had realized that he was the one man with whom she did want to spend her whole life. Then her fears and frustrations at the impossibility of her dreams had erupted in anger, and she hadn't been in the least reasonable. And finally, realizing what she was doing, she had just run away from it all, and from him.

Fighting with him hadn't gotten her anywhere. She'd just wanted him all the more. Now it was terri-

ble having him here. Having to see him. Having to feel
him touch her, brush by her...

Kiss her...

She trembled suddenly in the soft evening breeze.
She told herself that it had only gotten cold, and that
she was sitting on an empty seawall with nothing on
but her skimpy bikini. It had seemed perfectly respectable when there were dozens of other bikini-clad
women running around, but now, with the beach de-
serted, she felt bare and cold and ridiculous, sitting
there all alone.

She jumped down to the sand, then gasped out loud
when she realized that there was no sand. She had
landed in a foot of water. In amazement, she stared
around and realized that the tide had risen so high that
the beach had entirely disappeared. The sea came all
the way up to the wall.

"Oh, no!" she said aloud to herself. Her blanket,
her beach towel and her little canvas bag with her sun
block and a few dollars and—most importantly—her
key to the condominium, had all been left on the
beach. The no longer existent beach.

She started running through the shallow surf, hoping against hope that the tide hadn't risen so high all
along the shore. But it had, of course. When she came,
panting and shivering in earnest, to the spot in front
of Ryan's condo, there was still no sand to be seen,
only the darkening waves.

She swore softly again. The light was fading quickly,
and she could hardly see a thing. Goose pimples rose
on her arms while she sloshed back and forth in the
water, hoping that maybe her bag had sunk, and that
she would eventually find it.

But neither sloshing nor swearing did her a bit of good. She spent at least half an hour searching; then, exhausted and cold, she hopped back up on the wall.

It was just about dark. The moon had risen, and the sun was just about to sink into total oblivion. The wind had grown stronger, and she was cold and wet and she didn't have a key to get into her condo, or even a towel to wrap around her shoulders.

"Damn it!" she swore out loud. There was no one around to hear her. She turned around and stared at the condo. Someone had to be there. One of her aunts had to be staying with the children somewhere. Unless, of course, they had all decided to go out to dinner, too, taking the children with them.

No... someone had to be there.

She hurried along the wall to the white picket fence around the pool. She circled that and entered the parking lot, where she checked out the cars.

She didn't recognize a single one—except for Ryan's white Mercedes.

Groaning, she wandered back to the pool area and sank onto a lounge chair. Eventually someone would come back.

It was a nice night. She should enjoy it. The stars were just starting to twinkle like diamonds. It was really quite beautiful.

But it was as cold as Siberia! she told herself a moment later. She had goose bumps from head to toe, and her teeth were chattering. The ocean breeze wasn't pleasant at all; it was downright frigid.

She leaped up again, hugging her arms fiercely around herself. She decided that she would just start knocking on doors. She was related to twenty-five of the people staying here. Someone just had to be in one of those rooms!

But fifteen minutes later and feeling five degrees cooler, she still hadn't drawn a response. She had knocked on the door of every single condo occupied by a family member. And every single one of her relations seemed to have disappeared for the evening.

Having made that discovery, Lucia realized that she was terribly thirsty and her stomach was beginning to growl.

She could have endured all of those, she told herself. Maybe not with complacent fortitude, but she could have endured them all the same. It was the fact that she simply had to go to the ladies' room—desperately—that finally convinced her that she would have to break down and call on Ryan Dandridge.

She marched into the elevator, pressed the proper button and crossed her arms over her chest. When the elevator opened, she hurried to Ryan's door and banged hard, quickly, before she could even think about chickening out.

"Hey! Enough!" he thundered from inside; then the door flew open and he was staring at her, an irate scowl etched into his features. Wary surprise slowly replaced the scowl. "Lucia," he said blankly.

"Yes." He was still staring at her, blocking the entryway. She wasn't formally dressed, but he wasn't exactly suited up for company, either. He was clad in nothing but a cobalt-blue velour robe. Little tufts of hair teased at the V of the neckline and flourished on his hard, muscled calves beneath the hem of the garment. He examined Lucia from head to toe. He seemed to take in her crossed arms and scantily clad form, but apparently he didn't notice the goose bumps, because he didn't move aside.

"What do you want?" he asked her.

What if he had a date in there? she wondered in sudden panic. Maybe he *was* dressed for company.

"I want a key. I'm locked out!" she snapped. If the blonde was there, she just might die. Right on the spot. "Damn it, Ryan, I'm freezing to death! Would you please get me a key—"

"Lucia, there aren't any more keys. I gave them all out."

"What?"

"You have one, Dina has one—"

"And you don't have a backup key?"

"I did. I had two. But Joe has one, and your Aunt Faith has the other. Go see Joe. He'll let you in."

"I can't see Joe! Joe is out to dinner!"

"Oh, that's right." He paused staring at her. He scowled. "Why aren't you out with them, where you're supposed to be?"

"Because I—oh, never mind. Damn you, would you get out of the way, then? I'm freezing, and I—"

"And you what?"

"If you can't let me into my own apartment, I have to borrow your facilities, and if you have company, I'm sorry for the intrusion, but it's totally necessary!"

He burst out laughing. He seemed to see her at last, all of her, including the goose bumps that covered ninety-nine percent of her flesh. He cast her a mischievous smile and threw the door open wide, backing away from it. "Do come in," he said softly.

She stepped in warily. "Said the spider to the fly."

"Lucia, I'm not at your door—you're at mine," he taunted. But as she hurried down the hallway, she heard the door close with a sharp click. She spun around. He was leaning against the door, arms crossed over his chest, smiling.

"I don't have any company."

Why did she feel so vastly relieved? Whether he did or didn't, it was none of her business.

She was such a liar. She lied to herself constantly. She *did* care. Maybe things would be all right again once they were back in different states. Then she could bear the pain again. But while they were here, she couldn't help but care.

He started walking toward her, and when he stopped in front of her, he placed his palms very lightly against her cheeks. "You *are* cold," he said softly.

She couldn't move. She couldn't speak. She stared at him as he smiled down at her, tenderly, gently. Then the smile faded, and his hands dropped. He stepped away, walking toward the open door to his bedroom. He spoke to her over his shoulder in a flat, toneless voice. "I'll get you a towel and a robe. You're frozen. You'll get sick if you don't do something."

Lucia struggled to find her voice. "It really isn't necessary. All I need is—"

He was back, shoving a soft terry-cloth pile into her arms, his teeth clenched in fury. "Take them. Take the damn things and take a damn shower before I'm responsible for your having caught a case of pneumonia.

"I'm not—"

"Lucia, you're half naked as it is! Wouldn't it be better to sit around in a robe?"

"I wasn't going to sit around—"

"What were you going to do? Stand around outside? Where are the rest of your clothes, anyway? What were you doing out at this time of night in nothing?"

"I'm not in nothing! This is a perfectly respectable bathing suit!"

"There isn't a damn thing respectable about that bathing suit."

"Get off it, Mr. Dandridge!"

"Hey! *You* came to *my* door, shivering and half naked."

"I am not half naked."

"Three quarters naked, then."

"Let me use the crummy facilities and I'll take my three-quarters-naked body elsewhere!"

"The hell you will!"

Suddenly he was dragging her through his bedroom to the bath. She tried to pull away, startled by his fury, and dismayed by her own temper. She was just in the mood for this fight. She was really ready for battle.

Except that she couldn't win.

It didn't seem to matter. He wasn't going to let her get away, not until he reached the door to the bathroom. It was huge, larger than her own. There was a massive, glass-enclosed black tub in the middle, and she could see the stars through the skylight above.

He whirled her into the room, dropping the towel and robe on the floor. "Take a shower!" he snapped.

"You can't make me!"

"Want to bet?"

Her heart started to flutter painfully against the walls of her chest. They were both simmering, she realized, both keyed up for this. They were both caught in a turmoil of thoughts and emotions, standing on the edge of some dangerous precipice, in danger of falling at any moment.

She walked forward and picked up the towel and the robe. "Thank you," she said softly. "I think I will take a shower."

He stepped back, nodded stiffly, then turned around and left her.

Lucia watched him go and gasped for breath, unaware that she had barely dared to breathe until now. Then she remembered how desperately she had needed to use the facilities, and she began shivering again, eager for the heat of a sizzling shower.

The water was just that. She peeled off her bathing suit while streams of liquid heat poured over her. She smoothed the water over her face and felt like crying. She wanted to apologize. She wanted to explain that she barely knew what she was saying to him half the time, that it was just the way the words came out, burning with the heat of the turmoil inside her.

Suddenly too hot and unable to stay in the shower another moment, she groped for the door and slid it open. Somehow, while the water continued to fall, she caught her finger, and cried out in sudden pain.

"Lucia?"

The door to the bathroom burst open, and Ryan was standing there, his eyes wide, the pulse at the base of his throat beating raggedly. He stared at her as she stood in the doorway of the shower, naked and sleek, with beads of water dripping from her.

"Lucia..." he whispered, and then he was walking toward her. She watched him come, and she couldn't move, couldn't say a word.

He touched her, and she cried out again at the delicious feeling of his hands on her bare flesh. She laid her palms against his chest, meaning to push him away. Instead she slid her fingers along the inside of his robe, against his bare skin and the coarse, masculine mat of tawny hair that grew there. She came to the belt and tugged on it, loosening it.

He groaned softly and pressed his lips against the wet column of her throat, then kept them there for a moment against the whirlwind beat of her pulse. He curved his hands around the fullness of her breasts and knelt slowly before her.

Chapter 6

I thought you could keep your hands off me," she whispered, smiling.

"Oh, I can. I am completely immune."

"So am I."

"I don't want you at all anymore."

"I don't want you, either."

"Lucia?"

"What?"

"I'm lying through my teeth."

"Ryan?"

"What?"

"So am I."

"Lucia?"

"What?"

"Shh..."

There had never been a time for Ryan when it hadn't been magic to be with Lucia.

"I need you," he murmured. "I need you tonight, so badly."

She sighed softly and almost fell against him, but he held her, his fingers moving over the softness of her skin.

He'd known other women in his life, women he had liked, cared for, enjoyed and with whom he'd shared friendships. But he had always drawn a line at deep involvement; he had never been committed.

With Lucia, he had quickly become involved. He'd wanted a commitment; he had wanted to hold on to her forever. But he had promised no strings, which was what she'd wanted, so he'd never been able to tell her how he felt. He had tried so hard not to hold too tight . . . and she had run away anyway.

But the magic had stayed with him. He felt it now, touching her, feeling the soft touch of her hands on him.

She was a beautiful woman in so many ways. Now, surrounded by a fog of steam, she was utterly enchanting. She was a small woman, but surprisingly strong and lithe, compact and nearly perfect. Her skin was naturally golden, pure and sleek and as soft as silk. Her breasts were firm and full and beautifully formed. She was all lush curves and slim, exquisite angles, sensual, uniquely pure. Maybe the innocence was in her eyes, no matter how sultry their dark appeal. They were truly the mirror of her soul, large eyes, fringed with black lashes. They were fascinating pools. They made promises. They were wide and honest and compelling, and completely seductive. She was staring at him now, her lips sweetly sensual and slightly parted, but she didn't whisper a word.

He held her hips and drew her near, pressing his mouth against the silky smoothness of her abdomen. He could hear her heartbeat, and he could feel the sweet yielding of her flesh, of her self, to him.

He laid his cheek against her, feeling the whirling madness of his own heart. He wanted her desperately. It was probably wrong. She was in his apartment, naked in his shower, only at his insistence. He shouldn't be here. He should rise and walk away.

But he could never do so.

"Oh, Ryan..."

Her fingers fell softly on his hair, and he looked at her. Dark curls tumbled over her face and added haunting shadows to the dark mystery of her eyes. Her fingertips played softly against his skull as she stared at him gravely. And then he saw that her lips were trembling. He saw the blue vein against the long column of her throat where her pulse beat. He could not walk away from her.

"Lucia..." He wanted to say so much more, but there was absolutely nothing he could trust himself to say. He groaned softly and pressed his lips against her flesh again. He tasted that same flesh with the tip of his tongue, and he drew swirling patterns of warmth and heat, his tongue dipping into her navel. She cried out softly and fell to her knees before him. Her eyes met his, and then her mouth met his, and he brought his arms crushingly around her.

The shower beat on relentlessly, and the steam continued to rise around them, but they were both heedless of it as he drank of her, savoring her lips, her tongue, her mouth. His fingers trailed over her shoulders and along her spine to the small of her back. His hands curved over her buttocks and drew her tight against him. Tight against him...so flush that their bare flesh fused together, so that he felt every womanly nuance of her, so that she became aware of how desperately he had missed her, and how desperately he wanted her now. She slipped her hands slowly over his chest to his shoulders, shoving his robe until it fell away. She brushed her nails erotically against his neck and over his shoulder blades, then down his back to the rise of his buttocks.

He drew away from her and laid his lips against the hollow of her shoulder, then kissed her forehead, her eyelids, feeling the soft flutter of her lashes against his lips. He kissed her throat and the deep valley between her breasts, and then he kissed her lips again. A sweet simmering moved inside him. He met her eyes and felt their dark depths upon him in return. Her breathing came in sharp, shallow bursts, and her breasts rose and fell in a fascinating rhythm. He cupped them tenderly and gently, keeping his eyes upon hers all the while, feeling his own excitement skyrocket with the sensual glaze that touched the darkness of her eyes. He rubbed his thumbs slowly and deliberately over her nipples, and his hands shook as she swelled and hardened beneath his touch.

He rose, bringing her to her feet before him. She lost her balance and fell back, and he followed her into the rush of the storm, into the cascading steam of the shower stall. He pressed her against the wall and kissed her again, and the warm water fell upon them, soaking them both. He gazed down into her eyes. ''We can't stop now,'' he told her softly.

"No," she replied. They stood still for several seconds, droplets streaming over their faces. Then she gave a soft cry. Her hands wound around his neck, and she sought his lips again, eagerly, hungrily. Their mouths met and meshed and parted, again and again, and fever tore through him. He touched her cheeks, then brought his hands to her breasts again and lifted them to meet the sweet pleasure of his mouth. He ran his teeth and tongue over her honeyed flesh and the hard, darkened peaks, and then he bathed in the warmth and intimate wetness of her tongue again. With the water thundering down on his head and shoulders, he dropped to his knees again. He cupped her buttocks and brought her flush against him, then teased his fingers along the soft flesh of her inner thighs. He nipped and laved her, then ravaged her intimately with fevered tenderness. Soft gasps and incoherent sounds escaped her, and she fell down before him.

Their lips met again, and then the heat of the shower and the stars shining down on them through the skylight were simply not enough. The harsh, incoherent sound that came next was his own. He rose, lifting her into his arms, turned off the water and stepped from the stall. Water dripped from them both, but he barely noticed it. All he saw was the dark sensual beauty in her eyes, the longing and desire that matched his own. He saw the beauty of her naked flesh, and if he hadn't been so desperate to have her, he might have stopped just to savor and remember the sight of her in this bare and exotic state. She was so beautiful, meant for passion. Nothing was ever halfway about Lucia. She made love with all her heart and all her being, and he thought that perhaps that was what had finally won his heart, the incredible sensuality of her ability to give.

Still holding her, he fell onto his bed. Neither of them noticed that they quickly soaked the maroon comforter. Ryan moved his palm over her cheeks, ever fascinated by her eyes. Then he kissed her again, and their limbs intertwined, sleek and wet in the endless heat aroused by the friction of skin on skin. Ryan found her earlobe while her hands moved restlessly over him.

"I've missed you."

"And I've missed you."

"I've missed . . . this, too."

She hesitated, and then her voice came, as soft as a breeze. "I've missed . . . this, too," she echoed.

He rose above her, then whispered just above her lips that she was beautiful. He went on to tell her just what parts of her were beautiful. And she smiled beautifully, wickedly, as her fingers closed around him, and she whispered that he was beautiful, too.

He cast back his head and groaned with need and desire and triumph, and he rose high above her. Her legs, so long and supple, moved invitingly, wrapping around him. He moved his body very slowly, and very thoroughly, into hers, and he watched her eyes, as she watched his, and then the simmering within him bubbled and steamed over and he cried out again, crushing her into his arms. He no longer moved slowly, but he moved like the wind. He stroked her from within, the need in him so great that it was anguish, and the pleasure that he found within her so great that it was anguish, too. She held him with all of her, with the tenderness of her arms, with the soft tightness of her femininity.

He could not let her go. He brought her to a near frenzy, then slowed his rhythm until she moved frantically against him and he picked up the beat again. He shifted and moved within her, until at last he could hold back no longer. He cried out savagely and hoarsely, a sound that tore from the depths of him, and the essence of him filled her. And then sweet pleasure came raining down upon them as she cried out in turn. Stars seemed to burst in the velvet night and twinkle before his eyes, and then he fell down beside her, feeling her lie quiet in his arms, damp and delicious, still a part of him, for the moment, at least.

They were silent. The stars disappeared, and the night breeze slowly cooled their bodies as he drew her more closely against him.

He was probably going to have hell to pay. She had come here of her own accord, but he had been the one to suggest the shower.

He rose up on one elbow. In the light from the bathroom, he saw that she was staring at the ceiling, but he couldn't read what she was thinking.

"Lucia..."

She pressed her fingers against his lips. "Don't talk, Ryan. Please don't talk. Not now."

"Lucia, I don't want you being mad at me for what just happened."

"I'm not mad at you."

"Lucia..."

"I'm not mad at you, Ryan! I'm—I'm glad about what just happened. It was...I've missed you." Her eyes fell briefly, then rose to his again. "It's just so hard to be here and forget we had a past."

"Why did you run away?" he demanded softly.

She sat up, throwing her feet over the side of the bed and turning her back to him. He reached for her arm, dragging her back. "Lucia, damn it, I wasn't demanding anything from you."

"Drop it, Ryan!"

"Lucia—"

"Drop it! I am not mad at you, and I—I wanted this as much as you did. Maybe more. But please, for God's sake, don't ruin it with a bunch of words that can't do anything but hurt!"

He gritted his teeth. She looked at him, biting her lower lip, then rose. He jumped to his feet, cutting her off near the door of the bathroom.

"Where are you going?"

"To borrow your robe."

He stared at her stubbornly. "Stay with me."

"I can't."

"No words, no questions, no reproach."

"I can't!" she whispered, and her tone was desperate. "Ryan, my whole family is here!"

"Oh." Frustrated, he let go of her arm. She started to move away, but he pulled her back into his arms again, hard, until their naked flesh was flush again.

He loved her this way. He loved their lovemaking, but he loved to just touch her, too. To just be together, sleeping, daydreaming, idly lying beside one another, just touching.

He smiled very slowly, seeing her flush, knowing that it might be very easy to keep her just a little while longer.

"I understand," he said, holding her against him and feeling the fullness of her breasts against the hard muscles of his chest.

"Then—"

"Stay. Just a few minutes more. We don't know that anyone is even back yet. They're probably still out to dinner."

"A lot of time has passed."

"Then what's just a little bit more?"

"Ryan . . . this isn't right."

"It is right, Lucia. It's entirely right." He bent his head and kissed her. It was a new kind of kiss. It was slow and seductive and leisurely, and it was bestowed upon her with all the mastery he had acquired in his lifetime. It was hypnotic, demonstrating leashed passion and promising the fulfillment of all desire. His lips moved and trailed across her cheek to the lobe of her ear. He caught it between his teeth. "Please . . ." he asked.

"Please . . ." she repeated almost mindlessly.

"Stay!" he pleaded.

"Stay," she repeated. She rose on her tiptoes, her arms encircling him, her fingers playing at his nape. She pressed against him, and then she moved away just slightly, running her fingers down the length of his body, then enclosing them around him so that he shuddered. His eyes opened accusingly on her, and she smiled wickedly in return. "I *can* stay—just a little while longer."

He caught her, lifting her above him, and his eyes were sharp with longing and warning. "Damn right you're going to stay now!"

She laughed delightedly, her dark eyes ablaze, but then he touched her intimately, and her laughter died in her throat as she buried her face against him. He carried her back to the bed, and in seconds they were whispering to one another again, with their blood beating a wild, pagan rhythm, as if they were truly one.

And when it was over, they were both silent and sated.

Ryan felt as if he had died a little bit, as if all his energy had been spent in the tremendous explosion of his senses. He lay still, unable to move, her head resting on his shoulder. He closed his eyes, and she must have closed hers, too, because the two of them slept.

She woke later, and woke him. "Ryan, I told you that I had to go! It's 4:00 a.m. now!" She bolted up while he was still trying to awaken.

"Lucia, there's nothing to worry about—"

"Fine! Easy for you to say! You don't have twenty-five relatives residing in the same building."

"In the same building, Lucia, not the same room."

"The same room. Dina! She must be worried. She must be going nuts!"

"If anyone was worried, he or she would have come here by now. You and I were the only ones left behind, remember?"

"I haven't even got any respectable clothing. And I still don't have a key. I can't sneak back in quietly! Ryan," she wailed, "you are a louse!" Her dark eyes flashed dangerously. He started to laugh at her, and she slammed her palms against his chest. "Ryan, you don't understand!"

He captured her hands against him. "Lucia," he said, making an effort to restrain his amusement. "I do understand, honestly. But what if nothing had happened? What if you had come in here and had a shower, and we had both sat down in the living room and dozed off? It would be exactly the same."

She was silent, frowning suspiciously. He slowly, regretfully released her hands. "Grab your suit and put on my robe. I'll get dressed and walk you down, and we'll knock discreetly at the door. I imagine that Dina is there now, and that she isn't worried because she never looked into your room. I'm sure she assumes that you're in there sleeping."

Lucia kept staring at him.

"All right?" he insisted.

"Maybe I should go down alone."

"Lucia! At least you know me. I'm a friend of the family, or a friend of Joe's, at least. Do you want your aunts to think you've been out half the night wearing practically nothing with a stranger?"

She blinked, her dark lashes fluttering over her eyes. "I'm not sure."

"Lucia!"

"All right, all right. But hurry. It's so late." She turned around then and saw the disarray of her hair. "Oh! Ryan, where's your brush?" She groaned softly. "One look at me and anyone would know exactly what I've been up to!" she cried in dismay.

Ryan swallowed. She was right. One look at her and he *did* know what she had been up to...and he wanted her to be up to it all over again. He couldn't let her walk out of his life again. He just couldn't.

But for the moment he needed to get her back into her own room. He knew that she loved her family dearly, and that it wasn't fear or embarrassment that was driving her, but respect for their morals and beliefs.

He cleared his throat. "My brush is on the dresser. Just give me two minutes."

Lucia hurried to get the brush, but Ryan couldn't resist one last jibe. "Lucia!"

"What?"

"I love your hair like that!"

"Very funny!"

He hesitated. "I'm not being funny."

Within minutes he was decently dressed in jeans, a polo shirt and a jacket. Lucia had donned his robe, and he took her hand while they left his apartment and rode the elevator down to the second floor.

Ryan tapped softly at Lucia's door. There was no answer, and he arched one eyebrow, then tapped again.

"Darn Dina!" Lucia muttered, but just then the door opened and a very sleepy-looking Dina in an oversized T-shirt stood there irritably. She stared from Lucia to Ryan, trying to wake up, and then she looked at Lucia again.

"What on earth are you doing out there?"

"Trying to get in."

"I thought you were sleeping!"

Lucia smiled awkwardly. Ryan stepped in with an answer. "We were sleeping. Lucia lost her key, so she came up to my place to wait for you to come back, and we both dozed off."

"Oh," Dina said flatly. But she kept staring at Ryan, politely inquiring.

"Oh," he said, and smiled.

Dina liked Ryan a lot, Lucia knew. It was easy to like Ryan. But after the events of this evening, Lucia didn't appreciate the intimate little smile the two of them were sharing.

"Dina, I'm sorry I woke you up, but would you mind if I came in? It's very late."

"Sorry," Dina said. Yawning, she stepped back. Then she smiled at Ryan again. "Want some tea, some coffee? Espresso? Cappuccino?"

He shook his head. "Nothing, thanks. I'll see you two sometime tomorrow, I imagine."

His eyes fell on Lucia. Feeling them brush over her, she trembled, and it seemed as if her flesh came alive again, wanting him, even as she watched him walk away.

She would have loved to have stayed in his bed through the night, sleeping with him, their limbs entwined, their arms around one another. It had been so good just to touch him again....

The thought warmed her, and she suddenly needed very badly to be alone. She wanted to hug what they had shared that night to herself. She wanted to savor it in her dreams. She had remembered so much, and she had forgotten so much. Once it had all been hers. The fullness of the night, the sweet intimacy of his loving. Once it had been so easy....

And tonight it had been as if their time apart had been washed away. There hadn't been an awkward moment, only the beauty of being together, of touching, of being touched. She loved Ryan, and she loved what he did to her, and . . . there was no future in it.

Tonight she didn't care. She simply wanted to cherish the memory.

Dina was staring at her curiously. "How'd you lose your key?"

"Pardon?"

"Your key. How did you lose it?"

"Oh," she murmured. "I lost everything. I took a walk, forgetting that the tide would rise and wash my things away. I lost my key and my bag and everything."

"Oh," Dina said, nodding gravely.

"Don't nod at me like that!"

"Like what?"

"Like you don't believe me."

"Who said I don't believe you."

"It's the way you're looking at me."

Dina grinned mischievously. "Guilty conscience, cuz?"

Lucia groaned and headed for her room. She heard Dina locking the door; then she heard her cousin laughing softly again. "Don't worry, I won't mention the hour of your arrival to anyone."

"Dina, I did fall asleep—"

"Yes, I'll bet a man like that can be exhausting."

"Dina—"

"Good night, Lucia."

"Dina—"

"Hey!" Dina laughed. "Quit while you're ahead."

Lucia had to quit. Dina had stepped into her own room and closed the door. Lucia could still hear her laughing softly.

"Oh, God help me!" Lucia moaned.

She needed help. She realized that when she tried to sleep. Her memories were bright and colorful, keeping her awake, and though she cherished them, they were painful, too.

She just didn't know what to do.

When at last she did sleep, it was already morning.

When she awoke she realized that she had left her bathing suit in his apartment. She had other bathing suits, but the idea that it was in his apartment made her uneasy. She wasn't sure why—none of her aunts was going to go up and snoop through his belongings.

Maybe she just wanted to see him.

She dressed in a different suit and one of her oversize beach shirts, then left her room. Dina had left a note saying that she was already down at the beach.

Ryan might well be there, too, Lucia thought, but she decided to take the chance and try to see him. Maybe he had slept late, too. Maybe he was making coffee and orange juice, and perhaps she could help him make breakfast. They had done it that way all winter; he had done the eggs, and she had fried the bacon. Sometimes they had just had cereal, but she had sliced the bananas while he had poured the cornflakes.

It had been so nice to do things together. They had always talked while they prepared the meal. He had told her about his projects and asked her advice. She had explained restoration methods. They had talked about the president, about the state of the world, about anything and everything....

Dina would never have run away, Lucia thought. But Dina hadn't known what it was like to love him and wonder when he would leave her for the next woman who caught his attention. He had never lied. He had never even lived with someone before, as he had been living with her, even for that brief span of time....

Dina would have fought for him. And maybe she would have been right.

Lucia sighed, pushing the elevator button. She didn't want to analyze things at the moment—she just wanted to be with Ryan. This vacation wasn't so long that she could waste time.

She stepped off the elevator and headed for his door. She frowned, seeing that it was open a crack. There were loud, angry voices coming from inside, Ryan's—and someone else's.

She paused, standing by the elevator. She was interrupting something, she realized. She should head back downstairs.

It was Gino Lopez, she realized. She shouldn't be eavesdropping, but she didn't seem to be able to move. The men were shouting with total disregard for the fact that they might be overheard.

"You owe me!" Lopez thundered. It was a threat, Lucia realized.

"I don't owe you a damn thing," Ryan retorted. "I paid you back—"

"Yes, yes, you paid me back! But who else would have given a kid still wet behind the ears a loan like that?"

She heard Ryan exhale slowly, straining for patience. "You gave me the kind of loan that could have put me into your debt forever. You gave me the kind of loan that had killer interest attached to it. Because that's what you want, Lopez, to have your debtors owing you forever—and willing to do your dirty work just to stay alive and afloat. Well, I paid you back. I paid you back with the sweat of my brow and the labor of my own hands, and I hate the fact that I was fool enough to even get involved with you. And I won't do anything for you now. So just get off my property. I won't be threatened, or bribed."

"I could kill you!" Lopez threatened.

"Don't be a fool. You're getting to be an old man. If you touched me, I'd break your neck."

"My son—"

"Lopez, get the hell out!"

The argument was coming to an end, and Lucia didn't want to be caught standing where she was. She ducked quickly into the elevator and pressed the button for her floor.

Instead she found herself on the third floor, standing face-to-face with Theresa. "Lucia! I was just looking for you. There's a husbands' and wives' tournament at one of the courses today, and—oh, Lucia, I know that this is an awful imposition, but—"

"You want me to watch the kids. I don't mind at all."

"Dina is already down there, but I'd feel better if both of you kept an eye on them."

"Sure," Lucia said. "No problem." Theresa was still staring at her doubtfully, so Lucia kissed her on the cheek. "Go! The kids will be fine, I promise. Dina wouldn't let anything happen to them, and neither would I. Good luck, and have a good time."

There was a clattering on the stairs that flanked the elevator. Startled, Lucia and Theresa looked at one another. Then Theresa's eyes narrowed as she saw the figure disappearing down the staircase.

"Lopez!" she said. "What on earth is going on with that man? He's harassed everyone here!"

Lucia shook her head. Everyone including Ryan. She wondered what the man had wanted Ryan to do. She wished she had the nerve to go back and ask him.

But she couldn't go back up. She had just promised Theresa that she would get down to the beach and watch the children.

She kissed her cousin again. "Forget Lopez. Have a good time. Get going, okay?"

"Okay." Theresa gave her a dazzling smile and stepped into the elevator with her. When they reached the ground floor she saw Bill waiting for them anxiously. He looked at Theresa. "Is it okay?"

"It's fine, Bill. Go," Lucia said with a smile.

He flushed. "I'll make it up to you one day, honestly, Lucia."

"You don't need to make anything up to me. They're my cousins, and I love them to death."

He flashed her a bright smile. "When you have your own little army, Theresa and I will watch them for you. I promise."

"If she doesn't get started soon," Theresa teased, "we'll be too old."

"Watch it," Lucia warned. "You'd better go before you make me change my mind."

"Yes, watch it!" Bill warned Theresa. He grabbed her arm and dragged her to the car, waving to Lucia. Lucia waved back.

She watched them leave, then remembered that she didn't have a key. She ran quickly up to Aunt Faith's, garbled out an explanation about her lost key, then took her aunt's. She avoided more questions by saying she was watching the children, then hurried back downstairs and out to the beach.

It seemed that it was just her and Dina and the kids that day. Lucia kept watching the building, wondering if Ryan might come down. But he didn't appear, and she tried to quit watching for him, because Dina was watching her.

"Missing someone?"

"I don't know what you mean."

"Oh, Lucia! You're so transparent."

"I'm not missing anyone."

"I keep getting this feeling that the two of you have a certain chemistry."

"We do not."

"Aha! You see, you knew instantly who I am talking about!"

"Dina!"

Dina laughed and rolled over on the beach blanket. The twins, busy building sand castles, looked at her and shrugged to Lucia. Little Tracy, playing with a pail at Lucia's side, started giggling.

"Would you stop!" Lucia sighed.

"Sure. When you confess. You have met him before, right?"

"Dina!"

"Okay, okay, but just remember when you want to talk about it that I'm here."

"And that you're all ears?" Lucia asked her.

"Exactly."

At four o'clock Theresa and Bill returned for the kids, flushed and happy, because they had won the tournament.

Dina and Lucia congratulated them warmly, then watched the children go upstairs with their parents. Dina stood and yawned. "I feel like a sand pile. I'm going up for a shower. You coming?"

Lucia hesitated, then shook her head. "I'll be along in a few minutes."

Dina shrugged. "Whatever you want." Then she smiled knowingly. "Still waiting, huh?"

"I just want to swim without the kids for a moment, that's all."

"I'll take up your bag, huh? After last night . . ."

"Take it," Lucia said.

"Sure you're not ready?"

"I just want a few minutes alone."

"Sure," Dina said disbelievingly, but she collected her things and waved cheerfully—then winked.

Lucia groaned inwardly and waved her cousin on, then stood up and stretched, too. It was getting late. The colors on the horizon were beginning to change.

She *was* waiting for Ryan, she realized. She wanted to see if he would come down to the beach with her, now that she was alone.

She waited a few minutes longer, then walked down to the water. The distance wasn't very great—the tide was already rising.

She walked along the water for a while, splashing with her feet. It was warm and nice. She looked back to where she had been lying with Dina. Dina had already taken their things up, but there was someone else there now, stretched out on a towel with a newspaper

lying over his face. For a moment her heart beat
quickly and she thought it might be Ryan, but then she
realized that it was a much older man.

She walked slowly back, thinking that it might be
one of her uncles. She still wasn't sure—the paper
covered all of his face.

Then, as she got nearer, the wind picked up in a
sudden gust, and the paper was blown away.

It wasn't one of her uncles. It was Gino Lopez.

Lucia almost turned around and walked the other
way. Then she paused, thinking that there was something a little bit strange about the way he was lying.
She frowned, standing still as the surf encroached and
the night began to fall.

He was on a towel, and he was wearing bathing
trunks. His hands were folded over his stomach, and
he was staring straight up at the sky.

Straight up, his eyes wide and unblinking.

Lucia took a step closer to him. He was still staring
straight up. He hadn't even realized that his newspaper had blown away.

She took another step, and then she realized just
what was so strange about him, and why he was so
oblivious and unblinking.

He was dead.

She brought her hand to her mouth, holding back a
scream.

She had to call the police. She had to call the police
right away. She shouldn't be holding back her scream;
she should be screaming as loudly as she could.

But she didn't scream—she panicked in cold silence. It was almost night, and the beach was de-

serted. All that she could hear was the insistent pounding of the surf.

The police!

She still couldn't move. She realized very slowly that she was afraid, and not because Lopez was dead. She was afraid because she didn't know how Lopez had gotten to be down here, dead on the beach.

She delicately reached out a finger and touched him. He was ice cold and stiff, and she let out a scream just at the feel of him.

The police, the police, the police...

But Gino Lopez had been the nastiest sleaze in the entire world. He had fleeced countless people. Countless members of her own family.

"Oh, no!" she breathed out loud, shaking her head. No. None of them would have murdered Gino Lopez. No matter what Lopez was saying or doing or threatening, they wouldn't have killed him.

But they were such a close-knit group. What if one of her uncles had gotten furious on behalf of one of her other uncles? The family was so close and so important. No, they were not murderers! But what if it had been accidental?

Or what if... ?

Suddenly she heard the sounds of argument again in her memory. An argument she had heard just this morning between Gino Lopez—and Ryan Dandridge.

No... Oh, no!

She swallowed, afraid that she was going to be sick. There was a dead man in front of her, and either the man she loved or one of her dearly cherished relatives just might have done him in.

Ryan. She had to get Ryan. Whether he was guilty or not, she had to see him. She had to know. She had to bring him down to see the body. She had to get him to call the police.

She jumped up and hurried along the wall, then went racing past the white picket fence toward the elevator. She punched against the up button, but the elevator didn't come. She heard giggling.

"Hey, kids! Don't you dare play with the elevator!"

The giggles faded. Lucia sighed, wondering which of her little cousins had been guilty. She heard quick footfalls as the children ran away and, a moment later, the elevator appeared.

She stepped in and rode it to the top, then ran to Ryan's door and beat fiercely on it. It seemed to take forever and ever for him to answer. When he threw it open he was in cutoffs and a tank top. His eyes widened, then narrowed. "Lucia?"

"Did you do it, Ryan?"

"Did I do what?"

Lucia burst into the room and swung around to stare at him, her hands on her hips. "Did you do it?"

He shook his head, baffled. "Did I do what, Lucia? Did I take that blonde to dinner? Yes, I did. Guilty as charged. But—"

"Stop it!" she shrieked.

"Lucia, *you* stop it! Do you need a drink? Or have you already had a few too many?"

"I'm calling the police."

She hurried to the phone. When she picked up the receiver, he wrenched it out of her hands. His features were taut and wary and furious. "What the hell are you talking about?"

"Lopez!"

"Lopez?"

"Don't you dare act so innocent with me! I heard him threaten you today, and I heard what you said to him. And now he's lying down there on the beach. Dead."

"Dead?" he inquired very slowly, as if she had lost her mind.

"Dead! Deceased! Cold as ice. He's down there, I'm telling you! And you—"

"And I what?"

Lucia bit her lip. "We need to call the police."

He stared at her hard, then dialed the police emergency number and reported that there was a dead man on the beach. When he hung up the phone, he asked, "Happy? Now come on. We're going to go down and see him."

He grabbed her hand and dragged her in tense silence from his apartment to the elevator. He kept her hand in a deadly vise all the way down to ground level, and then all the way over to the wall, where he suddenly stopped short.

"A dead man?"

She looked over the wall. There was no blanket— and no man. There was nothing but water. The tide had come in completely in the time it had taken her to bring Ryan down.

"He was there!" she said, and pointed.

"Sure he was," Ryan said. She spun around, staring at him, and realized that he didn't believe a word that she had said.

Suddenly they heard the sound of sirens.

Ryan groaned aloud, leaning against the wall. "Great. I gave them my name on the report, not yours."

"He was there, I tell you!"

A black-and-white patrol car came sliding into the parking lot. Two tall officers got out of the car, then approached Lucia and Ryan. Ryan smiled at Lucia as a heavyset, grim-looking officer drew a notepad from his back pocket.

"Tell him all about it, Lucia," Ryan said softly, and he crossed his arms over his chest, waiting.

Chapter 7

The older officer was the one to speak first. "Ryan, you say you've got a body?"

Ryan shrugged and turned toward Lucia. "Lucia, this is Sergeant Mahoney. Sergeant, Ms. Lucia Lorenzo. She saw the body. I called in for her."

The sergeant's eyes fell on her accusingly. "A body, huh? Where is it?"

Lucia stiffened and indicated the beach. "It was there. It's gone now."

"Uh-huh."

Her temper flared. "Sergeant, I'm telling you the truth. There was a body on the beach."

"Lady, I'll bet there were a lot of bodies out on that beach today. Good weather draws them."

"A dead body, sergeant."

His partner came up behind him. He was a young officer, really young, without a single line on his face.

He stared at Lucia in fascination and smiled shyly. "Don't worry, ma'am," he said. "Lots of people kind of look dead, but then you know that they're alive 'cuz they just get up and walk away."

"Look," Lucia snapped furiously, "I am not a fool—"

"Ms. Lorenzo," Sergeant Mahoney drawled, "just how many dead bodies have you found in your lifetime?"

"None. I mean one. The one that I found—"

"And would you happen to know who the dead man was?" Sergeant Mahoney asked.

Lucia opened her mouth quickly, then closed it slowly. It was gone. The body was gone. Maybe she had been crazy. Maybe Lopez hadn't been dead at all, and maybe he *had* picked himself up and walked away before the tide came in.

Maybe the tide had washed him away.

Whatever had happened, wasn't it for the best? What if someone in her family had murdered Lopez?

No. None of them was a murderer! All right, what if one of them had accidentally killed Lopez? That sounded better. In self-defense. Lopez had put him or her into a life-threatening situation, and he or she had responded....

It couldn't have happened. It just couldn't have happened. But still, the body was gone. The tide was in, and the body was gone. It made no sense whatsoever to give the police a name for a body that didn't exist.

She looked up. Ryan was staring at her, his eyes narrowed. He hadn't offered the sergeant a name, either.

The members of her family hadn't been the only ones arguing with Gino Lopez. In fact, the actual death threats had passed between Ryan and Lopez. Ryan, who was staring at her, who was keeping his mouth shut, who was watching her, waiting for her lead.

Sergeant Mahoney was staring at her, too, as was his young partner. Her tongue seemed to grow thick in her mouth. She had never lied to the police before. She'd never had any occasion to do so. She couldn't seem to bring herself to do so now.

Ryan spoke up at last. "I don't think Ms. Lorenzo spent time inspecting the body for any identity, sergeant."

Sergeant Mahoney lifted one brow doubtfully. "Ms. Lorenzo, are you sure that there was a body—a dead body—on the beach?"

Yes, she was sure. Damn sure. But if they wanted to doubt her, it would have to be their problem. "There was a body there. But the tide has come in since I saw it."

"Perhaps you gentlemen could watch for a body washing back up on shore over the next few days."

"Sure, Ryan, we'll do that," the sergeant said. He was still looking at Lucia as if she were slightly addled. Even the younger officer, who had stared at her so flatteringly, seemed to doubt her sanity.

The sergeant shook her hand. "Nice to meet you, Ms. Lorenzo." Lucia was certain that he actually winked at Ryan. "And we'll keep our eyes open, Ryan."

"Thank you, sergeant. We're sorry to have disturbed you, but we did think—"

"It's our job to come out," the sergeant interrupted. Lucia clenched her teeth. It had been her own decision not to push the point. "Good night," the sergeant told them both.

"Good night," his partner echoed. He flushed a furious shade of pink. "It was a pleasure, Ms. Lorenzo."

Lucia smiled. "Likewise, officer, I'm sure."

The two policemen walked away. Neither Ryan nor Lucia spoke until the two men had climbed into their patrol car and driven out of the parking lot.

"Why didn't you tell them the identity of your corpse?" Ryan asked Lucia.

"Why didn't you?"

"I asked you first."

"I didn't tell them because you didn't tell them. You seemed to have some reason for not wanting to."

"Lucia, I never even saw a corpse."

"Oh! So you think I'm imagining things, too!"

Ryan turned around and leaned over the wall, looking down into the water. "The tide is high, but I'm not sure that it would have been strong enough to carry away the body of a full-grown man."

"Ryan, I'm telling you—"

"All right, all right."

"You still don't believe me!"

"Lucia, I believe that *you* believe you."

"What does that mean?" He sighed, and Lucia's temper flared. "Ryan, I asked you—what does that mean?"

"I mean that I'm certain you're convinced that you stumbled onto Gino Lopez, and that he was dead. But . . ."

"But?"

"Well, Lucia, it's true, you don't deal with corpses on a daily basis. Maybe it was Lopez, but maybe he was just sleeping, and when you came tearing up to my apartment, maybe he woke up and saw that the tide was coming and walked away."

She locked her jaw, staring at him. "Good night, Mr. Dandridge," she said stiffly. Squaring her shoulders she turned to walk away, but he caught her elbow, spinning her back.

"Good night?"

"That's what I said. And I didn't just *think* that I said it, I really did!"

"Amusing, Lucia, but—"

"The whole thing is just hysterical."

"Is it?" He held her arm tightly, watching her eyes. "You know, you never did answer my question. Why didn't you tell Sergeant Mahoney that the man you found was Gino Lopez?"

"Because..." She hesitated, lowering her eyes. She couldn't admit to him that she was afraid—just a little bit—that someone in her family might have been pushed to a point where they might have been responsible for the man's demise. She couldn't do it. She didn't really believe it, so she couldn't possibly say it.

On the other hand, Ryan could be as guilty as any member of her family....

"What difference did it make? They thought I was crazy. Why give them a name?"

"Is that the real reason?"

"This whole thing has been absurd. Of course it's the real reason. They didn't believe me, so why bother to go on? Now, if you don't mind..."

He shook his head. "I do mind."

Lucia stared down at her arm where he held her; then she stared into his eyes. Sometimes it just seemed so incredible that he was back in her life. But for such a short span of time...

"What?" she murmured.

"Where are you going?"

"To my room. To take a shower."

"And then?"

"What do you mean, and then?" Lucia asked carefully.

He smiled. It was the smile that had snared her from the very first. It was a satyr's smile, wicked and sensual, but it was warm, too, and filled with charm. "I'd like to ask you, Ms. Lorenzo, to have dinner with me."

"Dinner?"

"Dinner. It's a meal people eat at night."

"You're inviting me out? On a date?"

"What's wrong with that?"

"Nothing. Everything. Oh, Ryan, I don't know."

"My apartment. I'll cook. No, we'll cook."

"I—I don't know, Ryan. This doesn't seem right. I am telling you the truth. I found a body—"

"Lucia, what can we do? It's gone now."

"You still don't believe me, and you think that I should come for dinner?"

"I do believe you."

"You lie like a rug."

"Lucia, I am not lying to you."

She hesitated, staring into his eyes. She had waited for him all day; she had longed to see him. Last night had been a fantasy, and she wasn't sure that she could deny herself the opportunity to let the fantasy continue. She was still in love with him. With distance she could bear the separation. When they were in the same building, she simply couldn't.

"Do you really think that's such a good idea?" she murmured.

"I'm not thinking at all, Lucia. I'm asking you to be with me tonight."

"For dinner."

He shrugged and smiled again. "For dinner. And . . . whatever."

She had to smile in return. "I'll be up in an hour. Does that give you enough time?"

"An hour is perfect." He released her arm at last. She smiled vaguely; then her smile faded and she turned and headed for the elevator. He didn't follow her, but she felt his eyes on her. His gaze warmed her, and she suddenly felt a sweet trembling excitement racing through her. She didn't want to think, either. She just wanted this night. She wanted to bathe luxuriously and dress up and sip wine with him while they puttered around together in the kitchen. She wanted to eat by candlelight, listening to soft music, and she wanted to lie in his arms, and she was incredibly excited, knowing that the evening could end with the two of them making love.

It would all end soon enough. She didn't want to think. Tonight she just wanted to laugh, to feel.

The elevator brought her to the second floor, and she wandered toward her own door. Dina opened it. "Hey, there you are. Are you coming out to dinner with us tonight?"

"No."

"No? Lucia, now come on. You can't sit around by yourself every night."

"I'm not going to sit around by myself."

"Well, then?"

Lucia smiled sweetly. "I've got a date."

"A date?"

"A date."

Lucia went into her own bedroom. Dina followed. "A date?"

"A date."

"With Ryan Dandridge?"

"Yeah."

"Oh!" Dina sat on the foot of the bed.

"You—you don't mind, do you?" Lucia asked, suddenly worried.

Dina laughed. "Mind? Not at all. There always did seem to be something between you two. And I'm a family-oriented woman. If I can't have the man myself, I'll gladly see him with you. Wow. I am so glad!" She jumped up and kissed Lucia on both cheeks.

"Dina, I'm having dinner with him. I'm not marrying him or anything."

"Why not?" Dina teased.

Lucia reached into her closet for the dress she intended to wear and laid it out on the bed. "Ryan? Ryan doesn't want to settle down. He's not a commitment-type person."

"How do you know?"

"He told me so."

"All that—when he's just asked you out for a first date?"

"Dina..."

Dina stood up, stretching, then wagged a finger at Lucia. "There's more here than meets the eye, little cousin. But I'll let you off the hook tonight if—and only if—I get to hear all about it tomorrow."

"Sure."

"*All* about it. I want the juicy parts, too."

"Dina!"

"I'm leaving. If all else fails, we'll be at the smorgasbord, then at the hotel for drinks and dancing. And if he gets fresh, the aunts and uncles are all going to be playing whist at Mom's apartment."

"Is that a reminder or a warning?"

"It's whatever you want it to be!" Dina laughed. She winked, and left the room, closing the door behind her.

Lucia nibbled at her lower lip, then smiled. She wasn't going to worry about tomorrow. Not tonight.

She walked into the bathroom, peeling off her wet suit as she went, and decided to sink into the tub. A half an hour there, and a half an hour to dry her hair and primp. She was determined that it was going to be a very slow and luxurious evening.

In his penthouse apartment Ryan rummaged through the refrigerator and freezer, tossed a head of lettuce on the counter, Idaho potatoes in the oven and two New York strip steaks in the microwave to defrost. Then he glanced at his watch and determined that he had given Sergeant Mahoney and his young partner plenty of time to return to the station.

He picked up the phone and sat with it on the couch. First he dialed the number of the hotel where

Lopez had been staying. He asked for the man's room, and a male voice answered the phone.

"Is Gino there, please?" Ryan asked.

There was a slight hesitation. "No, I'm afraid he's out right now. May I help you?"

"Is this Ron?"

"Yes, who's this?"

"Ryan Dandridge. Your father came by to see me today. I've changed my mind about something. If he comes in, will you have him call me?"

"Sure. But you know him. I have no idea where he went, or when he'll be back."

"Right. But when he does come back, have him call me."

"Sure."

Ryan hung up. He hesitated a minute, then dialed the police station. Mahoney was back, and he came on the line.

"Joe, it's Ryan."

Joe Mahoney didn't answer right away. "What, more bodies?"

"Joe, this is serious."

"All right. Shoot."

"I just want you to take this seriously." He hesitated. "Lucia thinks she saw a man named Gino Lopez."

"So? Who's he?"

"Well, up in Boston he has a record longer than Pinnochio's nose. Loan shark, petty crook. He's been linked to a few mysterious disappearances and the like."

"Sounds like he'd be a suspect, not a victim."

"Yes, but men like that make enemies."

"Do you think that woman really saw him dead?"

"She isn't the hysterical type, Joe. Yes, if she thinks she saw him, I think it might be true. And he does sound like suspect material. But if he is dead . . ."

"Maybe the old geezer just went from a heart attack or something like that."

"Maybe. But I'm still feeling a little bit wary. Will you keep your eyes and ears open?"

"Sure. Can you give me anything else to go on?"

"Yes. He came down here with his son, Ron. You might want to check with the man and see if he knows anything about his father. I tried calling Gino, and Ron answered."

"You know this supposed corpse fairly well, then?"

"A lot of people know him fairly well. But not as a friend. Gino would have sold his own folks for profit." Ryan glanced at his watch. He wanted to shower and straighten up the place and set out some candles and open the wine so it could breathe. He wasn't sure why he had called Joe. He still didn't know whether or not he believed that Lucia had seen Gino dead. She'd probably seen him in a heavy sleep. But just in case he had been dead . . .

There was just a nagging suspicion that disturbed him. If Gino was dead, he might have been killed. And if someone had killed Gino and he or she thought that Lucia had seen him, it might be dangerous for Lucia. He just felt a little safer, talking to the police. Joe Mahoney was a good cop. He might have doubted Lucia's story at first, but if there was even an inkling of truth to it, then Joe would run it down.

"Joe, I've got to run."

"Hot date, huh?"

"Something like that."

"She's a beauty."

"Yes, she is."

"All your women are beautiful."

Ryan put the receiver away from his ear and stared at it with annoyance. "All my women?"

"Sure. Well, I'll get right on this, Ryan. I'll keep my eyes peeled, and I'll let you know if I hear anything."

"Thanks, Joe."

Ryan hung up the phone, but he stayed on the couch, frowning. Joe's words had disturbed him. And they weren't true.

Maybe they *had* been true—once. He had always thought of himself as a fairly even dealer. He didn't make promises. He hadn't ever been ready to settle down, and it seemed to him that a broken promise was a lot worse than one that had never been given. At first there had just been too much work. He'd worked construction by day to get himself through college by night. That was when he had fallen in love with architecture and building. There was something satisfying about working with his hands, but it was even more exciting to have a vision and see it through to completion. It hadn't been easy at the beginning. No one had wanted to lend money to a poor kid right out of college.

That, he reminded himself dryly, was how he had first met Gino Lopez. The banks hadn't wanted anything to do with Ryan, and he had heard through a friend that he could borrow from a nice guy named Gino. The interest rate had been exorbitant, but Ryan had been filled with confidence.

He had paid Gino back, too. But a year later, Gino had started asking him for "favors." Just little things. Once it had been a nephew who had needed a job. The kid had seemed okay, and Ryan had hired him. But then he had discovered him up on a steel beam, high as a kite on cocaine. Ryan had fired him on the spot, warning him that he had a problem he had to solve.

He hadn't minded trying to give a hand to Gino—Gino had given him a loan when no one else would. But he didn't owe Gino any shady deals. He was friends with most of the code inspectors in the city of Boston—but he was friends on an honest level. Gino had been threatening him now because one of the big new hotels that Gino had invested heavily in was about to be closed down for faulty construction.

The damn thing *should* be closed down, Ryan thought. It was an accident waiting to happen. Half the support beams in the place hadn't even been set to specifications. Ryan had told Gino so, but Gino just didn't give a damn. He was a dollars-and-cents man, and that was the final line. Gino Lopez wouldn't have cared if a whole floor had gone down, killing a hundred people.

If anyone deserved to be dead, Ryan thought dryly, it was Gino Lopez. But was he dead or not?

He didn't want to worry about Gino Lopez anymore. Not that night. Ryan leaped to his feet, found the white Bordeaux in the refrigerator and uncorked it, and headed for his bedroom and the shower. He paused, looking out at the night. The stars were rising high, and a half moon was out.

He opened the sliding glass door to the balcony and stepped outside. Far below the surf was crashing against the seawall. The air was fresh and fragrant with the sea.

He turned around, leaving the glass door open. He looked at the Jacuzzi and grimaced, then turned on the water to heat.

You never could tell....

Then he walked into his bedroom, determined to shower and dress quickly.

Under the steady stream of water, he quickly relived the past night. It had been magic; it had been hard to believe. He hadn't imagined that she might come near him. And he had never imagined that she might want him again.

Especially since she had seen him with the blonde.

Shelley. She was attractive, a nice woman, a schoolteacher from Iowa. It had been nice to go to dinner with her; it had been nice to walk along the beach. But he'd hardly been able to touch her, because he'd hardly been able to get Lucia out of his mind for more than two minutes. No one compared with her. No one laughed so easily, and no one had such sensuous eyes.

No one made love like Lucia.

He looked at his hands; they were trembling, and he wondered which one of them had made it all go bad. Maybe he'd been just a little bit afraid of her from the first. From that first moment when he had seen her and thought that she was the one, the one he had been waiting for all his life. The first time he had held her, the first time he had kissed her, he had been afraid of losing her.

She had meant so much to him from the very start that he had erected walls around himself, protective walls. And he hadn't even realized it. He'd tried to tell himself that he didn't want a commitment simply because he *did* want one, very badly.

He'd asked her to move in. And then one night, when things had run late with the architects he'd been working with in Newport, he'd come home to find that she wasn't in the least receptive to seeing him. He could remember it well, because she had promised him some fabulous Italian dish that night, and when he had tried to kiss her and ask about it, she had told him that he knew where the microwave was, and that he was welcome to help himself. Then she had curled up on a chair, watching television, not even looking his way.

At first he had taken it slow. He had tasted the food and praised it lavishly. Then he had taken a seat beside her, but when she had tried to squirm away, he had held her there and demanded to know just what was wrong with her.

She'd stared at him defiantly, wanting to know where he had been.

"Working late."

"So I heard. I talked to the secretary."

"Dorothy?" He frowned. She was a nice, quiet, sophisticated woman. Once, years before, they'd had a brief affair. He'd gone back to Boston, and she'd gone back to the prizefighter she had dated earlier.

"Dorothy," Lucia agreed.

"So?"

"Did you take her to dinner?"

No, he hadn't taken her to dinner. Barry Smith, Ted Nyler, Dorothy and he had all had fast food in one of the conference rooms around five o'clock.

He released Lucia, walking away from her. He poured himself a drink and stared into the fire. "No, I didn't take her to dinner," he said flatly, and walked into the bedroom.

A half hour later she came in. He tensed, his fingers laced behind his head as he stared at the ceiling in the darkness. His heart had begun to beat hard, his blood to race.

He heard her shed her clothing, and he felt her weight on the mattress. Slowly she climbed over him. Light flickered in from the hall, and his breath stopped. She was so beautiful. She straddled his hips, her head high and proud, her breasts full and round in the dim light, her hair falling softly around them. He held still, though, waiting for her to speak. Their eyes adjusted to the darkness and met, but she didn't say a word.

"I'm not the man for the third degree, Lucia," he told her softly at last. He wanted to reach for her. He wanted to forget that there had ever been a disagreement. He wanted to hold on tight for all his life, but he wasn't sure how to do so, and he wasn't at all accustomed to being questioned.

"Did you have an affair with her?" Lucia asked.

"Tonight? No."

"But . . ."

"Years ago."

"Are you—"

"Years ago, Lucia. At least six years ago."

"Ryan, just how many affairs have you had?"

He stared at her, clenching his teeth together tightly. "What difference does it make? We're together now."

"I can't help—"

"Lucia, I'm sorry. I worked late tonight. I don't know what Dorothy said to you, but it was an innocent evening. I had to work late, just like I said. I thought we were here together because we wanted to be together, not because we were looking to put choke holds on each other."

"Choke holds!"

She started to move away, but he caught her arm and pulled her back. Her eyes sizzled down into his. "Don't worry about a choke hold, Dandridge. I will never put a choke hold on anyone. I've been married, remember? And getting out of that mistake took years. I don't want to go through that ever again. But I don't want to live with you, wondering where the hell you are all the time, either. Does that make sense to you?"

"Lucia!"

"Ryan?"

It didn't make sense to argue, so he didn't let her do so any longer. He pulled her hard against him and kissed her, threading his fingers through the soft silk of her hair so that she couldn't escape him. He wrapped his arms around her tightly and held her so that her breasts were crushed hard against his chest, and then he rolled her beneath him and tried to communicate his apology and his promise into his touch. He had ended the argument. The night had spun into fantasy, but later, while he had watched the patterns of dawn falling across the room, he had remembered her words. She wasn't about to marry. He had known about her annulment; she always shuddered when she talked about it. But he had still thought that, living together, she would come to trust him.

Only she didn't trust him. Not at all.

That hadn't been the end of it. There had been an office party later that month, and lots of friends, his and Lucia's, had been there. She had spent a great deal of the night dancing with a young sandy-haired Lothario. He had gotten mad and practically picked her up off the floor to drag her out, and the fur and feathers had flown as soon as they got home.

She had no choke hold on him, which meant that he had no choke hold on her—that was her explanation for the evening. He told her that he couldn't change the past, but she was certainly capable of changing her behavior in the present. He couldn't remember ever being so angry in his life. And she had been furious, too.

And still they had wound up in one another's arms, and the volatility of their passion had been so great that it had left him trembling.

But the next day, when he had come home, she had been gone. All that had been left was a letter explaining that she had a life of her own, and she needed to get back to it.

The water still falling on his head, Ryan suddenly realized that the doorbell was ringing. He muttered an expletive, shut off the water and jumped out to dry himself. "Hold on! I'll be right there!" he called.

He ran into the bedroom and hobbled into briefs and a pair of chestnut trousers. He pulled a peach-colored knit cavalry shirt over his head, then paused, wondering if she had dressed up. He reached into his closet for a soft fawn-colored leather jacket, and decided he could be casual or dressy. He heard her knocking again. Barefoot, he started for the door, saw his wet hair sticking up in every direction and paused long enough to brush it. Then he flung open the front door, and she was there.

She was in a sea-green dress that fell just short of her knees. It was long-sleeved, belted and had a tailored collar, and it should have been almost prim.

It wasn't. It was soft and glorious, and it hugged her body. When she moved, the dress moved with her. It hugged her form, and she swirled and curved and drifted elegantly.

"Lucia," he whispered. She was wearing just a bit of makeup that night, soft mauve eye shadow that made the best of her haunting dark eyes. She smiled, glad of his reaction, and swept by him. She set her little black bag on the hall table and moved toward the open glass doors, sighing softly.

"Oh, Ryan, look at the night! It's just glorious, isn't it?"

He came up behind her, putting his arms around her waist, and nuzzled her neck. "*You* are just glorious this evening, Lucia."

She laughed a little bit nervously, spinning from his hold. Then she smiled, pointing at his bare feet. "You look wonderful. You smell wonderful. The outfit is great, but..."

"Hang on and I'll get some shoes." He laughed. "Pour yourself some wine—the bottle is on the counter."

By the time he came back she had poured them each a glass of wine and was in the process of breaking and washing the head of lettuce. He smiled at her, going to the microwave for the steaks.

"You always did make the better salad," he told her.

"No, not really. You're just too lazy to clean lettuce."

"Oh, yeah?"

"Um." She set the lettuce down and lifted her wineglass. She seemed a little nervous, he thought. "This is delicious."

"Thank you."

She smiled again. "You always did do the best job of broiling the steaks."

"That's because your attention span isn't long enough to flip them over while they're still rare." He pulled the potatoes out of the oven and stuck them in the microwave, then slid the steaks under the broiler.

"Well, I like that!" Lucia said indignantly.

He stood up, laughing. She started to protest, but he pulled her into his arms. "Don't you miss it?"

"Miss what?"

"Making love in the kitchen."

"We never made love in the kitchen."

"Want to try it now?"

"Ryan!" She started to laugh. Her fingers moved over the soft lapels of his collar, and he felt the swell of her breasts and the soft feminine flare of her hips against him. The temperature in the kitchen seemed to be rising unbearably. Her eyes, dark, sensual, compelling were locked with his. They seemed to seek, to search. They made him feel alive and vital; they made his pulse beat at a frantic rate....

She cleared her throat. "Ryan, you were talking about my attention span, remember? The steaks..."

"Oh! Oh, damn!" He wasn't going to get dinner made if he didn't watch out. He quickly drew the steaks out, flipped them, seasoned them and shoved them back under the broiler.

Lucia had gone back to the salad, patting the lettuce dry, then breaking it and tossing it into the bowl.

"Seriously, don't you miss this?"

She cast him a stare from beneath the shadow of her lashes. "Moments like this? Yes."

"Then come back."

"Come back?"

"Yes, come back and live with me again."

She was quiet as she found oil and vinegar and the proper seasonings and deftly measured them into the salad. He loved to watch her cook. She moved so competently. She never claimed that she did or didn't love to do so, but everything that she touched was delicious.

He loved to watch her do anything, he realized. Move, swim, run, walk...breathe. He just loved to watch her.

"I can't come back," she said. "You aren't even living where we were before, so how could I possibly come back?"

"Come to Boston."

"I work in Atlanta."

"You can work wherever you want to work. I know that. Everyone who deals in antique furniture knows your name."

"And the entire architectural and building trades know your name," she responded. "You could come to Atlanta."

"Is that an invitation?"

"What?" She paused, startled, her eyes meeting his. She almost poured out too much olive oil, but she caught herself in time.

"I said, is that an invitation?"

She tilted her head warily. "Why? Am I to believe that you would come?"

He grinned. "I really miss this."

"Making love in the kitchen?"

"We never made love in the kitchen, remember?" he teased her. He picked up the bowl of salad. Slowly. He had to learn to go slowly.

She watched him as he took the bowl out to the table. "Get the steaks," he told her. "No, never mind. I'll get the steaks and the potatoes. Want to light the candles? And put something on the stereo, please."

"Is this supposed to be a seduction?" Lucia called to him, lighting the candles.

"I don't know. Are you going to seduce me?"

"Well, you keep talking about making love in the kitchen."

"You brought it up the second time."

"Oh, did I?"

"Yes. Are you going to seduce me?" he asked her. He came out to the table with plates and silverware and napkins balanced beneath the plate with the steaks and potatoes. She ignored the question as she put something classical and quiet into the CD player. She came back to the table and helped him set everything out. She picked up her wineglass and met his eyes while she sipped slowly. "What was that?"

"I said, are you going to seduce me?"

"Oh, I don't know," she murmured, her expressive eyes searching out his once again.

He took the glass from her fingers and set it on the table. Then he kissed her lips with a lazy, leisurely sensuality, tasting her as if she were a part of the meal, ready to be savored. He felt the acceleration of her heartbeat as he touched her.

"You really do want to make love in the kitchen," she told him as he drew away slowly.

He shook his head, his lips nearly brushing hers. "I want to make love in the Jacuzzi," he said. She laughed, and for the moment the tension was broken. She moved away, and he pulled out her chair, then, like a French waiter, fixed her plate and poured her more wine.

He talked about his newest project as they ate, a turn-of-the-century shopping village on the Cape. He intended to invest in the restaurant himself. She talked about some pieces she had seen that would be great for just such a place. "Rustic? Fishing village, that type of thing?"

"Yes, exactly."

As she became enthused about his work, his heart seemed to hurt suddenly, banging against the walls of his chest. It had always been like this. They were good for each other. They fed off each other's enthusiasm. It was nice. No, it was more than nice.

She kept talking, then paused, aware that he wasn't really listening to her anymore.

"What's the matter?" she asked.

"Why did you leave me?"

She swallowed and shook her head.

"Lucia, why?"

She reached across the table, putting her fingers against his lips. "Don't, Ryan. This is just a dinner date, remember?"

"Lucia..."

She rose, and for a moment he thought she was going to leave. But she only walked toward the glass doors leading to the balcony, then she turned to him and smiled.

"Did you say the Jacuzzi?"

"What?"

"The Jacuzzi," she whispered. He didn't answer her, because she was still smiling, as she unbuckled the belt to her dress and tossed it to the floor. Then she undid the buttons, one by one. The dress slid from her shoulders. She slipped out of her shoes, shoving them aside with her foot.

She was in a sheer lace bra, panties, a garter belt and lace stockings. It was the most erotic outfit he had ever seen in his life.

Her eyes fell from his, and she bent her head over, dark hair cascading around her, as she undid a garter and skimmed away a stocking. It floated softly to the ground, and she paused, looking up. Her breasts were nearly spilling over the lace of the cups. Her smile became slightly wry.

"Well, it would help if you would kindly get naked, too. Striptease is not exactly my forte."

He stood, clearing his throat. "I don't know. You're doing pretty well as far as I can see."

She freed the other stocking and unhooked the garter belt, and it, too, fell upon the pile of clothing on the floor. Ryan slid out of his jacket and pulled his shirt over his head. She waited, watching him, smiling as his St. Christopher's medal fell back against his chest as he stripped the shirt away.

Then she slowly undid the front hook of her bra, and her breasts, honey-toned and full, the dusky nipples hard, spilled free. She slid her thumbs under the narrow strip of lace at her hips and peeled the bikini panties away.

He was just staring at her. "Hurry," she urged him.

He groaned. "Hey, you're the one who made me put the shoes and socks on." But they were already off. He grappled with his belt and tugged off his trousers and briefs, then strode toward her. She laughed like a vixen when he neared her, and scurried away, climbing up the steps and plunging into the Jacuzzi.

He followed her. They were in their own little world, enclosed by the balcony wall, the high rail and a latticework screen. He'd never felt so completely alone with her. The warm water sizzled and rushed around him. She was already seated on the circular ledge. He didn't pause, but went straight toward her, pulling her down into his arms. They faced one another breathlessly, feeling the steam and the rush and the heat around them, part of them.

He cupped and cradled her breasts, playing with them tenderly, passionately. She gripped his shoulders and closed her eyes, then pressed her lips to his.

She ran her fingers against the length of him. She teased his chest with her knuckles, then moved her hand lower. She encircled him, and he groaned softly and caught her buttocks, drawing her even closer. Gently he stroked her thighs, opening them. Holding her, he thrust inside her, strong and hard and sure. She cast her head back, crying out, and gave way to the sensation.

Time passed, but it meant nothing. They didn't speak, only made incoherent little sounds of passion. He moved her from her knees to a ledge, and, later, lifted her high above him and watched the provocative movement of her breasts. Millions of stars seemed to fall on him, but each time she would have left him, exhausted and sated, he drew her back and touched and kissed or teased her into arousal again, loathe to let her go.

And finally, when they were both too exhausted to move, he held her against him in the tub, and they both felt the lulling rush of the water and the softness of the steam, and they simply stayed that way together, staring up at the sky and the stars and listening to the surf. Ryan held her against him, his hand beneath her breasts. He was content to feel her legs dangle with his. Content to hold her. He'd never known such a sense of peace.

"Oh, Ryan, this is beautiful," she murmured.

"You're beautiful," he told her.

"You're beautiful." She laughed in return.

"Lucia—"

"Don't ask questions tonight, Ryan, please?" she implored him. If only her eyes weren't so expressive!

"Just one."

"What?"

"Can't we be together while we're here?"

"We—we are together."

His arms tightened around her, and his voice came out like a growl. "I want to be with you again tomorrow. I'll have breakfast, lunch and dinner with your family if you want, but I want to be with you. And I want some time alone."

She was quiet for a moment, and he was afraid. He was startled at how much it hurt to imagine that she might refuse him again. He thought that he had gotten over the pain, the thrust of the knife. Maybe this was wrong. Maybe it could hurt every bit as badly all over again.

But then he saw that she was smiling. "You really want to make love in the kitchen, huh?"

He smiled back, brushing her cheek with his knuckles. "Right."

She started to laugh, but then she noted his watch. "Ryan, it's 3:00 a.m. I've got to get back."

"Why?"

"I told you, my whole family..."

He sighed, rising. "Okay. If you think it's bedtime, I understand. But, Lucia..."

"What?" She was already out of the Jacuzzi, shivering in the night breeze. He reached for towels and threw one to her.

"Lucia, I'm sure that all your aunts are aware that people can have sex at 9:00 a.m. as easily as they can have it late at night."

She made a face at him. "Ryan, try to understand—"

"I do." He smiled. "Let's get dressed. I'll walk you down."

At the door to her apartment, he kissed her. She stayed there, bemused, waiting for another kiss, but he only pushed the door open. "Go to bed. You need your beauty rest. Remember, tomorrow we make love in the kitchen."

Lucia smiled, stood on her toes and kissed him again. She loved his smile. Lazily, he waved to her and started walking toward the elevator.

She walked into the hallway, flicked on the light and locked the door. It had been a nice night. No, a wonderful night.

She entered her own room, closing the door behind her. She still felt as if she were floating on clouds. Every bit of her flesh was probably eternally wrinkled from their extended stay in the Jacuzzi, but that was all right. She felt wonderful. She felt as if there was hope.

Maybe, just maybe, if she didn't run, they could have a future. She was so in love with him, and it was just so good to be with him....

She undid her belt and dropped it on the floor, kicked off her shoes and started on her buttons. She pulled her dress over her head, and, still in a tired, dreamy state, pushed open the door to the bathroom.

She flicked on the light and stared into the mirror, smiling at the wild disarray of her hair. It was a good thing she hadn't run into anyone!

Suddenly something she saw in the mirror disturbed her. A dark shadow in the bathtub.

She whirled around to look, and a scream bubbled to her throat, then died. There was a man in her bathtub. A dead man.

Gino Lopez, still in his swim trunks, still with his eyes wide open, was lying in her bathtub.

The scream finally tore from her, loud, shrill and hysterical, and she turned and ran from the room in terror.

Chapter 8

When Lucia reached the hallway she remembered that Dina was in her room. She couldn't leave her cousin alone in the condominium with a corpse.

"Dina!" Lucia ran to her cousin's room and threw open the door. But Dina wasn't there.

Lucia tried to tell herself that a corpse couldn't hurt anyone. Corpses were dead. It was the person who had made someone into a corpse who had to be feared.

Logic didn't help. She didn't need to save Dina, so she ran out of the apartment. It was dark, and very quiet. Lucia looked nervously around the balcony, aware that she was clad only in her lacy underwear, garter belt and stockings. She looked like an escapee from a striptease show.

It didn't matter. There was no way in the world that she was going to go back into her bedroom with the corpse of Gino Lopez.

None of her relations was about; no one had heard her scream. She looked up, toward the penthouse, and ran for the elevator. When it delivered her to the top floor, she raced to Ryan's door and pounded on it.

A second later he flung it open. His brow arched as she burst into the apartment, sweeping by him. "Lucia—"

"It's back!"

His eyes flickered over her attire, and he shook his head in confusion. "It's back? Lucia, what's back?" He stared at her as if the night had become too much for her, as if her mind had gone over the brink.

"Don't you stare at me like that, Ryan Dandridge. It. The corpse. Him. Gino Lopez. There's a corpse in my condo."

"In the condo?"

"In my room—in the bathtub!"

"All right, come on, we'll go check it out." He was in one of his terry robes. He turned toward the door, then paused. "Shouldn't we, er, get you a robe or something? You didn't want to be caught staying up here. I imagine you would just as soon not have one of your aunts wake up and pay a late-night call when you look like a dance-hall girl. What are you doing dressed like that? Or, rather, undressed like that?"

"Ryan, there's a corpse down there! I do not worry about my state of dress when dead men are lying in my bathtub!"

"All right, all right."

"Please, get me a robe! Then call the police, and then let's go!"

He walked into the bathroom and returned with a short man's robe. He handed it to her, watching her gravely as she slipped it around herself. Lucia stared at him indignantly. "Ryan, call the police."

"Let's call from your condo."

"You don't believe me!"

"I just think we ought to make sure the corpse is still where you think it is."

"There's no tide in the bathtub, Ryan!"

"Let's just call from there."

Lucia clenched her teeth tightly together. "Ryan, I'm telling you—"

"Lucia, I believe you. But let's go down, huh?"

She started to speak, then snapped her mouth shut. She stiffened her shoulders and walked out of the apartment ahead of him. He followed her calmly, pressing the button on the elevator, watching her covertly.

"Ryan Dandridge, I have *not* lost my mind, and there *is* a corpse in my bathtub."

"All right."

"Don't humor me!"

"I'm not humoring you!" They stepped into the elevator, and he pressed the button for the second floor, then glanced her way. "Where's Dina? You didn't just leave her sleeping there, did you?"

Lucia shook her head impatiently. "She's not back yet. Or she wasn't, anyway."

Ryan glanced at his watch. It was almost four, Lucia knew. She smiled sweetly. "Dina likes to party."

Ryan just nodded. The elevator came to a halt, and she stepped quickly along the hall. The door to her condo was still gaping open. She stopped suddenly as she reached it. "You first."

He smiled and stepped around her. "Lucia, a corpse can't hurt you."

"Just get in there, will you, please? Maybe you should have brought a gun or something."

"You want me to shoot a dead man?"

"No, damn you, Ryan, just get in there!"

He looked as if he was about to smile, and if he had, she would have hit him. But he didn't smile; he walked into the hallway, and she followed. The door to her room was still open, too, and he entered. Lucia followed him into the room, then paused. She didn't want to go into the bathroom again.

"Lucia?"

"What?"

Ryan came to the doorway of the bathroom and leaned against the frame, his hands in his pockets. "Lucia..."

"What? Damn you, Ryan, what?"

"Come here."

"No!"

"Lucia, there's no one in here. No one, nothing."

She stared at him blankly for a minute. "That's impossible!" she cried. She moved to the doorway and pushed past him, entering the bathroom.

The bathtub was empty. There wasn't a sign of another person—living or dead—in sight.

She turned and stared at Ryan. He was watching her in silence, but with definite skepticism.

"I'm telling you, Ryan, he was here!"

"Well, he's gone now."

"He was here!"

"Okay, Lucia. I believe you."

"I'm not staying in this room."

"You're welcome to use mine."

Lucia cast him a withering glare. "I can't, and you know it."

Ryan started to speak again; then he paused. They both heard Dina humming as she neared the condo.

"What do we do?" he asked Lucia.

"About what?"

"Your corpse. Tell her, don't tell her, what? It's up to you. We can call the police, except that we still don't have the body to turn over to them."

"I don't know..."

"Hey!" Dina called. She came around to the door of the bedroom. She was holding her high-heeled sandals by the straps and smiled at them sweetly; then she slowly observed their attire and laughed huskily. "Am I home too early...or too late?"

"Neither," Lucia said. Ryan was still staring at her. The look in his eyes demanded to know what she wanted to do.

"Well, it does look like it might have been an interesting evening," Dina said, amused.

"I came back ages ago," Lucia murmured.

"Um. The party moved downstairs, huh?" Dina teased. "Well, I like the cocktail attire. Matching terry. It's great. Just great. Can I fix you two something? Coffee, tea, a nightcap?"

"Dina, it's four o'clock."

"Coffee, then? Are we late for the night, or early for the morning? What's going on with the two of you? I can come back later. Of course, I'm not really sure where I can go now that I've come back, and it is four—"

"Dina, we don't want you to go anywhere," Lucia said. She stared at Ryan. She didn't know what to do. She didn't want to upset Dina with a story about a now nonexistent corpse, but she was also extremely nervous. She wondered if Ryan even believed that the corpse had been there in the first place.

"Coffee," Ryan said.

Lucia jumped. "What?"

He smiled at Dina. "I'd love some coffee. Sure you don't mind making some?"

"I don't mind at all. This is incredibly intriguing," Dina said. Her eyes fell with amusement to Lucia's robe; then she turned and headed for the kitchen.

"What are you doing?" Lucia demanded in a hoarse whisper.

"I'm waiting for you to decide what *you* want to do."

"Help me!"

"I'm trying to help you. It's just that there isn't a corpse here. Anymore." He added the last word like an afterthought.

Lucia wanted to throw something at him. "It was here!" she hissed.

"All right, it was here. I'll call the police—"

"No!"

"No? I thought that was what you wanted. And you might feel more secure—"

"No, because I intend to call them the second I find the corpse the next time!"

"Oh, Lucia! What if there isn't a next time? Come on, this whole thing—"

"Gino Lopez is dead, and I have seen him. Twice. I've seen his corpse twice. It was here!"

"Shh—"

"Don't you dare tell me to—"

But she did hush as he inclined his head toward the door. Dina was back. Ryan smiled at her. Lucia smiled, too. Dina shook her head with bemusement. "What on earth is going on here? Ah...I've got it. The age-old battle of the sexes. Lucia, don't torture the man. Either do or don't, but if you're set on don't, I suggest that you quit running around in your underwear. It's cruel. Ryan, cream and sugar?"

"Black," he said.

"Black," she repeated sweetly. Lucia stared at her, thinking that she'd like to throw something at her cousin.

"How about some doughnuts?" Dina said.

"Sounds great," Ryan agreed.

"Good." Dina started to leave them again.

Ryan called her back. "Dina."

"Yes?"

"Er, don't worry on my account. She already did."

Lucia gasped. Dina started to laugh.

"Good for you. Good for you both." Then she was gone again.

Lucia whipped the pillow off the bed and threw it with all her might at Ryan. He caught it, laughing and came toward her. She struggled, but he put his arms around her and brought her to sit beside him at the foot of the bed. Then she saw that his expression had grown serious.

"Lucia, you have to make up your mind. What do you want to do?"

"I don't know!" she wailed softly.

"I'll call the police—"

"No! Really. I don't want them to think I'm crying wolf. The corpse is definitely gone. But, Ryan, how did it get in here?"

He shrugged. "There's no sign of a forced entry."

"How many keys are there to this place?"

"I told you, four."

"Dina has one, Joe has one, and now I've got the one Aunt Faith had before. And the key I originally had washed up on the beach in my bag...somewhere."

"Maybe. Maybe you just forgot to lock the door."

Lucia didn't remember. She shook her head in frustration. "Ryan, I can't sleep here tonight."

"It's almost morning."

"I still can't sleep here."

"I told you, you're welcome in my room—"

"No!"

"If you're scared, maybe Dina will trade rooms with you."

Lucia thought about it and decided that would be her best chance for what remained of the night.

"There are two dead bolts once you're both inside," Ryan said. He smoothed back her hair, smiling. "When I leave, lock the bolts. Then I'll know that you'll be all right."

"You don't believe me," Lucia said bitterly.

He sighed. "I believe that you believe—"

"Oh, damn it, don't start that!" Lucia moaned.

"Okay, okay."

"Coffee's on the table!" Dina said cheerfully from the doorway.

Lucia stood quickly, trying to wrap Ryan's robe around her with more dignity. She smiled to her cousin. "Great."

Ryan rose, too. "Great," he echoed.

The three of them sat down at the table, and Ryan reached for a doughnut. Dina just kept staring at them. "All right, what's going on here?" she finally burst out.

Ryan almost choked on the doughnut. He recovered quickly and offered her a charming smile. "Illicit sex," he explained innocently.

Lucia groaned. She glanced Ryan's way, and Dina sighed.

"Lucia, please?" Dina asked.

Ryan and Lucia stared at one another; then Lucia looked at Dina. "I think there was a corpse in my bathtub."

"The corpse of Gino Lopez," Ryan elaborated.

Dina looked from one to the other. She pleated and smoothed her napkin, then said, "Oh."

Lucia and Ryan looked at one another. "That's it? Oh?"

Dina looked at Lucia. "It was there—but it's gone?"

"And it was on the beach the other day, too," Lucia said defensively.

"Oh," Dina repeated.

"I'm telling you the truth!"

"Ryan, have you seen this corpse?"

"Uh, not yet."

"Dina!"

"Well, Lucia, it is strange. Okay, I believe that Gino Lopez might be dead. Lots and lots of people hate him—" She broke off, her eyes going very wide and meeting Lucia's. "Oh!" she exclaimed softly, and Lucia knew that her cousin was sharing her own fears about the family and Gino Lopez. "Oh, no! No way. Our family might have had their problems with the man, but they wouldn't—"

"No, they wouldn't!" Lucia agreed fiercely.

"They wouldn't!"

"We know they wouldn't."

"Then who?" Dina looked slowly to Ryan, and Lucia followed her cousin's gaze. Ryan threw his hands up. "Oh, no!"

"No, no, of course not!" Dina said guiltily. "I mean, we still haven't even got this corpse, right? Oh, Lucia, I am sorry. I'm really not doubting you—"

"I can't possibly sleep in that room tonight."

"I'll take your room." Dina hesitated. "I mean, you didn't find him in the bed, right?"

"In the bathtub."

"All right."

Ryan stood. "You can still call the police."

"So that Sergeant whatever-his-name-is can laugh at me?" Lucia demanded. "Not on your life."

"But, Lucia—"

"No. I'm certain."

He was watching her with a curious mixture of concern and humor...and tenderness.

And disbelief, she thought resentfully.

"Ryan, if the police came, my aunts and uncles would surely see them, and everyone would be concerned, and we'd destroy a vacation that everyone waited for for a very long time. I'm all right."

"All right, then. I'll leave. You two lock up. And remember, if you need me, I'm only a phone call away."

Dina followed Lucia as she walked Ryan to the door. There was no way to say anything more. Dina stood right behind Lucia, hugging her arms around her chest. Ryan cleared his throat, but Dina didn't seem to notice.

"I've got an idea," Ryan told Lucia softly.

"What?"

"Let's take a long ride tomorrow. We'll drive down to the Boone Plantation and take a walk around the grounds, then head south to Charleston for the day."

"I . . ." She hesitated. Dina was right behind her. "Maybe we're getting a little bit too involved here," Lucia said. She knotted her fingers behind her back. She was mad. She must be losing her mind. There had been a corpse in her bathtub, and she was already worrying about her relationship with Ryan Dandridge again.

Ryan . . . who had fought with the corpse when the corpse had still been a living man.

Ryan . . . with whom she would love to go to Charleston. To spend the day strolling on the battery, sampling seafood, admiring old houses.

He touched her cheek. "Give me this, Lucia. Give me the little bit of time we have here."

Her fingers trembled behind her. "Charleston," she murmured.

"Is that a yes?"

"Sure. I'm a Southerner. I love the South. If a Yankee suggests a day in Charleston, how can I refuse?"

He smiled and pulled her close, then remembered Dina. "Excuse me," he told her, and then he kissed Lucia. He kissed her full on the mouth, slowly, tenderly. He parted her lips and gently teased the sweet inner recesses of her mouth, then released her. His eyes were warm as they met hers. "Good night, Dina," he said, still looking at Lucia.

For once Dina was silent. She barely waved when he left, and she didn't have a single thing to say about the kiss.

"Lopez," she murmured as Lucia locked the door. "Both bolts, Lucia."

"I've got both bolts."

"Maybe I'll sleep on the couch."

"Why don't we both sleep in your room?"

Dina shivered. "Sounds good to me. Only change into something else, okay? I'll feel really strange sleeping next to you if you come to bed in those garters."

Lucia managed to laugh. "I'll get something floor length in flannel, okay?"

"Okay."

Ten minutes later they were both dressed in long nightgowns. They had decided that they would leave the lights on in the condo, even though it would be daylight soon enough.

When they stretched out in bed, they were both silent for a long time. Lucia knew Dina wasn't sleeping, though. She could see her cousin staring at the ceiling.

"I shouldn't have told you," Lucia said.

"Yes, you should have. I knew something was wrong. And since you seemed to be doing okay with Ryan..."

"Dina..."

"I should be jealous, you know. I did see him first."

Lucia hesitated. She couldn't bring herself to tell her cousin about the past. Not then.

"I'm not really jealous. I'm only teasing. But tell me—is he just fabulous?"

"Er, yes, just fabulous." So much so that she was asking to be crushed all over again, Lucia thought.

Dina sighed. Then she shivered suddenly and rolled over. "Lucia, seriously, you don't think—"

"No, I don't think."

"But Dad was fighting with Lopez just the other day."

"Everyone fights with Lopez. He's that kind of man."

"I suppose."

"Dina, I know that our family is innocent."

"Yes, so do I. But, Lucia, your folks aren't here."

"I know your dad, Dina. He wouldn't hurt anyone."

"But they're so close. All of them, the aunts and uncles. What if Lopez was threatening one of them? That's the way we are. You know, we can say or think things ourselves, but if anyone else threatens, we all jump into the fray. We just don't allow others to hurt us. You don't think—"

"No. I don't think!" Lucia said firmly. Then she said it again, with even more conviction. "No, I don't think! Because no one in the family would have put that corpse in my bathtub! No one would want to frighten me."

"Right," Dina agreed. "Right!" She was quiet for several seconds. "Unless..."

"Unless what?"

"Unless they just didn't have any other place to put it."

"Oh, Dina!" Lucia wailed. "Let's just try to get some sleep."

"That's right, you're going to Charleston tomorrow." She giggled. "Today." Dina hesitated again for a minute. "Oh, no!"

"What?"

"You won't be back until late."

"So?"

"I'm not coming in here alone tomorrow night."

"You can stay up at Ryan's place, I'm sure."

"Oh." Dina thought about it for a moment. "Okay, just so long as I don't have to come in here alone!"

"Let's go to sleep."

"Fine."

They both closed their eyes. Suddenly there was a loud tapping on the door. Dina screamed. Lucia jumped out of the bed, her eyes wide.

"Lucia, Dina! Are you two up?" Aunt Faith called.

"Oh, my Lord, it's just my mother!" Dina sighed.

Lucia started to laugh, walking toward the door.

Dina moaned, pulling the covers over her head. "Ignore her and she might go away."

"Hey, do any of the Three Graces ever just go away?" Lucia demanded. "They just weren't bred to give up. I'll let her in."

"And act innocent."

"You bet," Lucia agreed.

They didn't have to do much acting. Aunt Faith was full of enthusiasm. She had found a good restaurant where they were all going to go to dinner the next night. And Uncle Mario was headed off to the golf course, if anyone wanted to join him. It was a beautiful day, and the kids were already down at the beach. Faith cheerfully kissed them both, never imagining that they hadn't slept all night, and wished them a good day. She was going to go shopping with Hope and Charity. They were going to make a day of it.

When she was gone, Dina and Lucia sank into chairs, looked at one another and started smiling, then laughing.

"We have to be crazy," Dina said.

"Have to be," Lucia agreed.

"Well, at least you get to go to Charleston."

"I should invite you, huh?"

"Not on your life. I wouldn't want to get into the middle of this. I'll go down to the beach. Maybe I can get some sleep there."

"Go grab a shower. Then I can get started."

"You're going to have a great date, falling asleep on Ryan all day."

"I won't fall asleep."

Dina showered and dressed in a bikini, then assured Lucia she wouldn't leave the condo until Lucia was ready, too. Lucia showered, using cold water, hoping it might wake her up. It seemed to do the trick.

She dressed in white shorts and sneakers and a light cotton blouse, then decided to throw a knit dress into a bag and bring a pair of high-heeled sandals in case they decided to stop somewhere for dinner. She and Dina left the condo together, locking the door carefully behind them. They went up to Ryan's together—Dina wanted a key to his penthouse.

Ryan was awake and expecting them. He was dressed in a casual cotton shirt and white shorts, which made his tan look marvelous. Despite a night without sleep he seemed amazingly rested and handsome. He said he would be glad to lend Dina his penthouse for the day, and that she should make herself at home. He gave her a key, and then he and Lucia were on their way.

"Tired?" he asked her once they were in the white Mercedes and heading south.

"No, not really," she said, flashing him a quick smile.

"You can lay your head on my lap, you know."

Yes, she knew. It would be easy to rest against him, easy to find comfort in his arms. Too easy.

"I'm all right," she said.

But she wasn't. She stared at the road for a while, then felt herself growing cross-eyed. She blinked, but the road didn't seem to straighten out.

Ryan set his hand on her nape and threaded his fingers through her hair, massaging her scalp. Her eyes closed again. "Lie down," he encouraged her softly.

"Just for a minute . . ."

She laid her head on his lap while he drove and wondered just how many times she had ridden with him this way. She wondered why they had ever fought. . . .

Then she didn't wonder about anything anymore, because she fell asleep.

What finally awakened her was the fact that she couldn't feel motion anymore. She opened her eyes slowly. She was on Ryan's lap, and his hand was resting on her hair, and when she first saw his eyes, they were filled with an intensity of emotion that startled her.

His lashes fell swiftly, and when they lifted again, the emotion was gone. His expression was bright with humor, but some of the tenderness remained.

"Hi," he said.

"Hi." She struggled to sit up, automatically smoothing back her hair. "We're here, huh?"

"The Boone Plantation. I'm sure you've been here before, but it's a nice place to visit."

"I slept the whole way. I'm sorry."

"You're cute when you sleep."

"Oh, yeah?"

"And, even better, you're silent."

"Hey!"

"Just kidding." His knuckles brushed her cheek. "Come on, let's go."

"Wait, wait—"

"Your hair," he said, laughing. "Go on, brush it out."

She did, and then she slid out of the car and he laced his fingers through hers.

It was a beautiful day, and there weren't many tourists around. Ryan paid their entry fee, and they took the tour through the house, listening to the history of the Boone family, the rise and fall of slavery and tobacco and cotton. Lucia had been there before, as had Ryan, but it was fun to come together. Old houses were something they both loved.

When they were done at the house, they walked down to the water, then around to the front of the house.

Lucia stared down the long drive and smiled at Ryan. "This is where they filmed parts of *Gone With the Wind*, you know." She pointed down the drive, which was flanked on either side by double rows of beautiful oaks. "Twelve Oaks—Ashley's plantation," she said.

"I know," Ryan told her. He shook his head teasingly. "I wonder what Scarlet ever saw in Ashley."

"Tradition, maybe," Lucia said softly.

"The concept fares rather poorly in my mind."

"You haven't got a romantic bone in your body."

"Every bone in my body is romantic," he assured her; then he laughed, taking her hand as they passed by the slave quarters and walked along under the oaks. "Scarlet spent eleven years of her life chasing an absurd dream, when she had Rhett right there all the time."

Lucia laughed. "She just didn't know what she wanted."

"Do any of us?" Ryan said softly.

"Yes."

"Tradition?" he asked her.

They paused near the paddocks, where a mare ran by with graceful abandon, followed by her foal. The sun fell through the trees and kept them warm, and Lucia leaned against the fence and stared at him. "Tradition? Yes, it is important to me. My family is important to me."

"Then why—" he began, then broke off, shaking his head impatiently.

"Why what?"

"Never mind."

"Ryan..."

"Never mind. Let's drop by the gift shop quickly, then head south, or we won't have any time in Charleston."

He had already turned and walked away. She had little choice but to follow him.

In the little shop Lucia bought T-shirts for the children, and Ryan bought them all facsimiles of Colonial dish and ball games. Lucia watched him thoughtfully. "You didn't have to do that," she told him when they were back in the car.

"I know I didn't have to. I wanted to."

"You like children?"

"Very much."

She stared straight ahead. Then, after a moment, she murmured, "When they're someone else's children and you get to hand them back when you're done playing?"

"Is that how you feel, or are you asking me how I feel?"

"Pardon?"

"Is that—"

"I love children."

"So do I. It's that simple," Ryan said. "Well, maybe not in herds of a hundred or more, but on any normal level, I love children."

Lucia smiled slowly. He reached out his hand, and their fingers joined.

As soon as he was driving again, the motion made her sleepy. "It'll be a while till we reach the city. Rest again," he offered.

"How can you be so wide-awake?"

"I'll pay for it tomorrow. And I went right up and fell asleep on the sofa. I'm willing to bet you and Dina stayed up talking."

"We did."

"Was she all right?"

Lucia hesitated. She wondered if she dared to tell him that Dina was afraid, too—not for her own physical well-being but that someone they loved might be guilty.

"She was...all right." Ryan grunted, and Lucia stared at him. "You know, you're awfully calm about all this."

"Lucia, I haven't seen him yet," he reminded her quietly.

"You don't believe me!"

"I do believe you. I just didn't find the corpse in my bathtub, that's all."

"All right. But, Ryan, the corpse *was* on the beach, and it *was* in my bathtub."

"I did call the police the first time, you know. And I would have called them last night."

"Um. And they would have laughed. But I warn you, you're all going to be sorry for not believing me—really believing me. Gino Lopez is dead, and every day that his corpse remains missing is going to make it harder for the police to determine how he became a corpse in the first place."

Ryan was silent for a moment. "Isn't that what you want?"

"No!"

"Lucia, I know what you think."

You don't know the full extent of it! she thought. But that wasn't really true. She couldn't believe that Ryan was a murderer any more than she could believe that one of her uncles was. It was just that the nagging fear was always there.

"I don't think anything," she lied.

He squeezed her fingers. "I don't want you to think anything," he said. "Not today, okay?"

"Okay."

"No past, no future, just today."

She looked at him. His eyes were shielded by his thick lashes, but he seemed to be staring at her intently. "Just today," she said softly.

Fifteen minutes later Ryan found a parking space right on the Battery, the promenade that looked out on the water, the islands and the old fort. Lucia paused, looking out to sea, as he locked the car. Fort Sumter lay beyond them, in the harbor.

Ryan came up behind her, placing his hand on her back. He pointed out to the fort. "Did you know that General Beauregard, the Confederate commander who was ordered to fire on Fort Sumter, had once been one of the union's Major Robert Anderson's instructors?"

Lucia turned and smiled at him. She shook her head. He turned again, indicating the beautiful old homes behind the green park. "Imagine everyone decked out in their Sunday best to see the boys in gray blow the damned Yankees from their native soil. They watched from their roofs and balconies. Major Anderson held out as long as he could, then surrendered when further struggle seemed futile. The only soldier who got killed was a Union boy who was struck by a Union shell within the confines of the fort. And then the Confederates were ordered to honor the Yankees as they evacuated. They were all gentlemen, or so they say." He lifted Lucia's hair from her neck and fluffed it around her shoulders. "They believed in tradition. In God and home and honor and family."

"They're good things to believe in," Lucia said softly.

He grinned and took her hand. "Come on, let's explore some houses."

In the end they didn't go into any houses, choosing to avoid the tourist haunts. Together they just walked along the streets on the Battery. Once, right across the street from the water, Ryan paused. "Now that's a beautiful house," he said.

Lucia agreed with him. It was Federal style, with a massive porch and wonderful tall white columns. There was a widow's walk on the roof, as if the original occupant might once have lived in a New England whaling village and remembered how it felt to stand so high up, looking out to sea and waiting for a lover to come home.

Ryan glanced at Lucia. "Four bedrooms. Three baths. A library—untouched, I'm certain. There's a carriage house around back, converted to a garage. What do you think?"

She laughed and studied the house. "Three big bedrooms. The master bedroom is a suite—during the Civil War, the master kept his books right off his bedroom. He hated to leave his wife to work. She was beautiful, and he was madly in love with her."

"Ah. But he went off to war—a navy man—and never came back."

"And she paced the widow's walk for years and years, always believing that her beloved would return to her."

"More likely she paced the widow's walk for about fifteen months, then turned around and married her husband's best friend."

"You're not romantic at all!" Lucia accused him, and he laughed.

"I just know women," he said.

"Oh, really?"

"I know what they tell me," he said pointedly, and she flushed. She lifted her chin in the air.

"You don't know women at all, Mr. Dandridge. You just think you do."

"Really?" His eyes were speculative.

"Uh-huh."

He gripped her hand suddenly. "Let's go find out."

"What?"

"Let's go find out. We'll just knock on the door—"

"We can't!"

"We can. I'm willing to bet that whoever owns this house is a history buff, and that they'll be more than willing to help us if we explain how much it would mean to us to know."

"Ryan, you can't just walk up—"

"Sure, I can." He shrugged and released her hand, then sauntered past the hedges and along the tiled walkway to the massive porch. "Coming?" he called to her.

"No!"

He shrugged again and knocked on the door.

Lucia stared at him in amazement. A moment later she saw the door open, but she couldn't make out the person standing in the doorway.

Ryan turned back to her. "Sweetheart, come on in. Mrs. Merriweather will be happy to show us the house. She needs to think about our offer, though."

"What?" Lucia mouthed.

"Sweetheart!" Ryan said again.

Lucia walked up the path to join him. She saw a very old, fragile woman standing in the doorway. She had marvelous pale-blue eyes, a wrinkled face and a sweet smile.

"Mrs. Merriweather, my wife, Lucia," Ryan said.

Lucia started to cough, and Ryan patted her on the back. "She's from Atlanta. She still isn't accustomed to good sea air."

Mrs. Merriweather laughed with pleasure and extended her hand to Lucia. "Hello, dear. Do come in. Your husband has been telling me that he's anxious to buy the place. I hadn't thought about selling, but I'd just love to have you to tea." She raised her voice slightly. "Mary, we have company for tea. Do come in, Mrs. Dandridge."

Lucia stared at Ryan, ready to throttle him.

"It was the only way to get us in," he whispered.

"You lied to that lovely old woman."

"Don't you want some tea?"

"I don't want you lying about this!"

Mrs. Merriweather, who had started into the house, paused. "Is there a problem, Mrs. Dandridge?"

"Lucia, please, Mrs. Merriweather."

"Lucia. What a lovely name."

"There's no problem," Ryan said. "My wife just hates to impose."

"Oh, no imposition. I shall enjoy your company. Please."

Lucia stepped into the beautiful old house with Ryan's arm around her.

Chapter 9

The house was charming, right out of a novel. They were welcomed into a large entryway with a marble floor, an overhead chandelier and a sweeping staircase leading to the gallery above. The ceiling was high, and the walls were light, and there were matching huge bay windows with velvet-covered seats on either side of the door.

Mrs. Merriweather was a traditionalist, Lucia saw quickly. The furnishings were beautiful antiques. There was a fine mahogany sideboard against the far wall, while the entryway chairs were early Victorian.

"How lovely!" Lucia murmured.

"Really, you must come up and have tea," Mrs. Merriweather said delightedly.

Lucia stared at Ryan, who shrugged.

Mary made her appearance then, coming down the stairway. She was an attractive redhead in a white nurse's uniform. She flashed Ryan a smile, and he smiled back. Lucia elbowed him in the ribs. "Shape up, Mr. Dandridge. Wives don't care for flirtatious husbands," she whispered.

Mary hurried down the stairs. Mrs. Merriweather introduced them all, then led Ryan and Lucia through the high arched door to the left. They came into a study with shiny hardwood floors and rows of books against the front wall, and tall open windows to the rear, their sheer white drapes blowing in the breeze. The windows looked out over a gorgeous pool.

"It's wonderful, isn't it?" Mrs. Merriweather asked, following Lucia's gaze. "My brother put the pool in, in 1934. It was so delightful when the children were here. But then his son was killed in World War II, and we lost young Thomas in Korea, and it's been just me ever since, I'm afraid."

"We really shouldn't impose—" Lucia said.

"Nonsense!" Mary said firmly from behind her. Lucia whirled around. The young nurse was carrying a tray of tall glasses filled with iced tea. Mint sprouted over the top of them. "Mrs. Merriweather is thrilled with your interest."

The old woman nodded, taking one of the glasses. "Of course. Not just anyone can appreciate an old place like this."

"Ryan..." Lucia paused, helping herself to an iced tea and thanking Mary. "My husband is a builder, Mrs. Merriweather. He works on new structures, and he also does reconstruction and preservation work on old homes and buildings."

"How wonderful," Mrs. Merriweather said. "Do sit down now, please. Mary, stay here with us. Maybe you can remember a few things that I can't."

They sat down, and Ryan guessed aloud that the house had been started in 1835. He was close, Mrs. Merriweather was pleased to tell him. The original Merriweather had come south from a Maine fishing village in 1830, and he had started the house two years later. Fishing had been their trade then, until the war, and then the Merriweathers had become blockade runners. "First, of course, they watched the shelling of Fort Sumter from atop the widow's walk. Cecilia Merriweather left a fascinating diary of the time. They had a party at the house that night. They were so full of optimism! Charleston was a beautiful city, then as now. Hot as Hades in the summer, but so lovely in spring. There are shells in the house—a cannonball stuck in the roof. We're ever so lucky that so much of the city is left—the North blamed South Carolina for the war, you see. We were the first state to secede. When Sherman made his march to the sea, we were lucky that he didn't head straight for us and raze Charleston to the ground. But he didn't, so this wonderful place of American heritage is still here. Oh dear, I seem to be wandering. Cecilia was my grandmother. My father was born upstairs in 1865, right when everything was falling apart for the South. They say that Cecilia paced the widow's walk, waiting for her husband to come home."

Ryan and Lucia glanced at each other quickly.

"Did he come home?" Ryan asked.

"Never. His ship was sunk in a naval battle off Newport Mews, and he never came home again."

"And Cecilia?" Lucia asked sweetly.

"Cecilia? Oh, she never remarried," Mrs. Merriweather said. "She raised her son and kept her property free from the Yankee carpetbaggers—oh, do excuse me, young man. You have a New England accent, and I mean nothing against you."

"No offense taken," Ryan said, smiling.

Mrs. Merriweather looked at Lucia. "You're from the South."

"Atlanta," Lucia agreed.

"A fine city," Mrs. Merriweather said. She patted Ryan's knee. "Of course, I'm sure that you come from a fine city, too."

"Boston."

"Ah. Yes. Another bastion of tradition."

"A Yankee bastion, but a bastion," Ryan said. He set down his tea and rose. "Mrs. Merriweather, could I impose on you for the use of a phone?"

"Of course. Mary, if you would be so kind...?"

Lucia frowned, watching as Mary led Ryan from the room. Mrs. Merriweather didn't seem to mind that the stranger she had invited into her house wanted to use her phone. Indeed, she seemed pleased about the entire afternoon. "Mrs. Dandridge—"

"Lucia, please."

"Yes, yes. Lucia, please come with me. I'd love to show you the garden surrounding the pool. And there are some wonderful outbuildings here. We have the carriage house, of course, and the old kitchen. And there's the caretaker's house, a charming cottage. It's a wonderful property, really."

"Oh, it is," Lucia agreed. She followed Mrs. Merriweather out a rear door and into the garden, then paused, looking back. What on earth was Ryan up to?

There was a tiny room for the phone beneath the winding staircase. It held a carved Edwardian seat, a Tiffany lamp and an old brass phone. There were no push buttons, so Ryan spent a few minutes talking to the operator to assure himself that he would be charged for the long-distance call to Myrtle Beach, not Mrs. Merriweather.

Finally he reached Sergeant Joe Mahoney. "It's Ryan Dandridge. Did you find anything?" he asked.

"Ryan, yes. I sent a man over. We found prints all over the place, but none that I can trace. I'm sure they must belong to Ms. Lorenzo and her cousin, and to you, perhaps. None of them belong to Lopez. He has a record, and we were able to draw up the information on the computer."

"Is that it?" Ryan asked, disappointed.

Joe sighed over the phone. "There was a dark hair in the tub, but, Ryan, we'd need something to compare it with. An awful lot of people in this world are dark-haired."

"And nothing else? No fibers, no clues?"

"Yes, we found a cotton fiber, but that's the same thing. Half a million pieces of clothing are made of the same kind of fabric. There was nothing to suggest that a murder had taken place in the tub—"

"The murder didn't occur in the tub. The *body* was in the tub."

"I'm sorry, but there was nothing to indicate a body was there, either. But . . ."

"But what?"

"Well, we can't seem to locate Gino Lopez alive, either. The son is getting very upset. He's filed a missing-persons report."

"Has he now?" Ryan murmured.

"He came in last night. He says he can't imagine where the old man has gotten to. He's very concerned."

"Then Lucia's right."

Joe was very quiet.

"What's wrong?" Ryan demanded.

"This girlfriend of yours, you think she's on the level, don't you?"

"Of course!"

"I mean, you don't think maybe she did away with this guy herself and is trying to throw off suspicion? She's the only one who ever seems to see this body, you know."

"She's also five foot two and probably no more than a hundred and five pounds, Joe. How do you think she could possibly drag around a body like Lopez's?"

"How do we know the body was ever dragged anywhere?"

Ryan felt his temper beginning to steam. "Joe, I guarantee you, Lucia did not murder Gino Lopez."

"And how can you guarantee that?"

"Because I know Lucia Lorenzo."

"That's what Mr. Monahan said about Mrs. Monahan."

"And who the hell are the Monahans?"

"Well, Mrs. Monahan killed her husband's brother, and while he was busy saying she couldn't possibly have done it, she was busy putting a bit of arsenic into his morning coffee...every day. So it's hard to say, Ryan."

"Joe—"

"All right. I'm not making any accusations. I was just asking, that's all. What about the rest of that group? Don't they all know Gino Lopez?"

"Sure. And I know him, too. He's been a slimy character for years. Dozens of people would probably like to kill him. But that doesn't mean anything."

"Hey, don't get defensive on me. I don't even have a body yet!" He paused. "I'm sorry I didn't come up with anything more."

"Well, thanks for the effort." Ryan hesitated for a moment, frowning. "Joe, no one saw your man go into the apartment, did they?"

"No, he was as discreet as a mouse. No problem. She'll never know you were checking up on her."

"I wasn't checking up on her, Joe. I was just trying to keep her safe."

"Has anyone threatened her?"

"No."

"Then what are you worried about?"

"I don't know. I just don't like it. Well, I guess there's nothing else to do for now. I'll check with you later."

"Sure thing, Ryan."

Ryan slowly replaced the receiver. When he stepped out of the little room, Mary was waiting for him.

"Everything all right?"

"Yes, fine, thanks. I didn't mean to take so long. Is everything all right out here?"

"Fine. Mrs. Merriweather has your wife outside. They're inspecting the outbuildings and the pool area."

"She isn't really my wife."

"No?" Mary said.

"Long story."

"I thought you were engaged last time you were out here. That's why I thought you wanted the house."

Ryan shrugged. "Well, I thought I might be getting married last time I came here. But she left me."

"How could she do such a thing!" Mary protested indignantly.

"She managed." Ryan laughed. "She thinks I just barged in here today. I had time to swear Mrs. Merriweather to secrecy, but I'm glad you didn't give me away, either. I'm taking a second stab at it."

"Good for you. She's beautiful."

"Yeah, isn't she?"

"But then, you're pretty great yourself."

"Thanks."

"If she gives you a hard time again, make sure you come to me for some consolation."

"I'll do that, Mary. Oh, where do you think I should take her to dinner?"

"Di Martino's is on the water and—"

"Nothing Italian." He grinned. "Her family can make the best Italian food in the world. I don't want to compete."

Mary laughed. "Marshall's. It's on the water, too, and their fish is superb. I'll make a reservation when you leave. What time?"

"Eight. We still have to drive back tonight."

"I'll take care of it."

"Thanks. I guess I'd better get back out there. Oh, and I'm going to buy the house. One way or the other."

"That's wonderful. Mrs. Merriweather will be very happy."

"I hope so. And she'll have the carriage house for the rest of her life, rent free. She knows that, right?"

"Yes, and she's touched. I hope things work out for you."

"So do I." Ryan gave her a thumbs-up sign.

Mary opened her mouth, then closed it, then decided to speak after all. "It's none of my business, but—"

Ryan grinned. "She's just not the marrying kind."

"Has she said so?"

"Yes—quite clearly."

"Um. But then, you do the same thing, you know."

"I do what?"

"Well, you give the impression of being a die-hard independent. Maybe if you sat down and really talked..."

"We've talked before."

"Sure, but maybe you were both on the defensive. It's frightening to be hurt. To love someone more than that someone loves you. Maybe if you take the plunge, maybe if you dare say that you really love her...maybe then she'll have the nerve to tell you back."

"I don't know," Ryan said thoughtfully.

"I'm serious," Mary said.

"Think the beach beneath the stars would be a good place to talk?"

"Anywhere is a good place to talk. Sometime when you're alone, when all the right words can be said."

"I'll work on it," Ryan promised her.

Impulsively, Mary kissed his cheek.

Ryan heard a slight sound and turned around. Mrs. Merriweather and Lucia were standing in the doorway. He was certain that Lucia had seen the kiss, though her eyes betrayed nothing as she stared at them. It didn't bode well for the evening.

"I've shown Lucia the outbuildings. I've even tried to talk her into staying for dinner, Mr. Dandridge, but she simply won't budge on the issue," Mrs. Merriweather said.

Lucia was staring straight at him. "I feel that I, at least, have overstayed my welcome," she said sweetly.

It was time to leave, Ryan decided. He thanked Mrs. Merriweather, winked at Mary and escorted Lucia out.

She pulled her hand from his the moment they reached the sidewalk. "Don't you ever do that to me again!" she snapped.

"Do what?"

"Tell someone that I'm your wife."

"Why not? What else was I supposed to do? Tell that lovely old lady that I was interested in seeing her home for myself and my mistress?"

"I'm not your mistress, either."

"It's a horrible, archaic term, isn't it?"

"Ryan, stop it."

"All right. My occasional live-in lover."

"I am not—"

He stopped on the street, catching her hand, swinging her around. "Then what are you, Lucia? Just what are you?"

She jerked her hand away and stared at him, her eyes smoldering with a deep, dark fire.

"I don't know. Just what is Mary?"

"A friend."

"A friend? You form your friendships rather quickly, don't you, Mr. Dandridge?"

"Lucia, let's not fight."

"Look, Ryan, I don't want to fight, either. That's why I'm not your mistress or your occasional live-in lover or whatever it was that you wanted me to be! I don't want to give you the third degree, or put you in a choke hold. But I'm afraid I find it humiliating to see you with another woman when—"

"I wasn't with another woman!"

"She kissed you."

Maybe, just maybe, Ryan thought, she was a little bit jealous. And that was a good sign. "Lucia—"

"Take me home!" she snapped. Her hands were on her hips, her head was tossed back, and her hair was cascading down her back in dark, lustrous waves. Her eyes were stormy, and he smiled suddenly.

"What is so amusing?"

"You really are gorgeous when you're mad."

"I'm not mad."

"And you're jealous, too."

"I am not. I just want—"

"We have dinner reservations at eight."

"Ryan Dandridge, I will not go to dinner with you."

"Yes, you will."

He reached for her shoulders, and she stiffened, trying to pull away. He didn't care. In full view of at least half a dozen tourists, he pulled her to him.

"Ryan Dandridge, don't you dare—"

He silenced her with his lips. They met hers with a fierce passion and with tenderness, and he kissed her as if they hadn't seen each other in decades, as if he were desperate for the taste of her. He kissed her until her hands went slack against him, until she went still and breathless.

Until she forgot her protest.

When at last he lifted his lips from hers, she inhaled in a gasp, her glazed eyes on his, her lips still parted and moist. He wished that they weren't in Charleston. He would have given his right arm to be alone with her, and he called himself every kind of fool in the world for wanting her so desperately.

"I've met Mary before," he said out of nowhere.

"Oh?"

"And I've met Mrs. Merriweather before, too. I didn't just walk off the street and into her house."

"Oh?"

"I thought about buying the place before. I saw a write-up about it in a magazine. Mrs. Merriweather didn't really want to sell, but she has no heirs. I came to see her, to promise her that if she sold to me, she would have the right to live on the property for the rest of her life. She's still thinking about it."

"So why did you tell her I was your wife?"

He shrugged. "I panicked, I guess."

"Um, I'll bet you did," Lucia murmured.

"I made dinner reservations. Will you have dinner with me?"

"Is that what you were doing on the phone?"

"What?"

"The phone call. Is that what you were doing on the phone?"

"Oh. Of course."

"I, er..."

"It's not quite five. The reservations aren't until eight. Maybe we should rent a room, rest, shower and change."

"Rest?" Lucia asked suspiciously.

He nodded gravely.

She was in for trouble, Lucia thought. But wasn't that what she wanted?

Half an hour later they were in a lovely room overlooking the park, and Lucia couldn't pull herself away from the window. She stared out over the cannons and statues, over the oaks covered with Spanish moss and out to sea.

Ryan was in the bathroom shaving, with the door open.

"It's really a gorgeous city," she called to him.

"Yes, it is."

"But very Southern. Even a Yankee can see that."

He popped his head out the door. "What are you, Ms. Lorenzo? The Italian Scarlet O'Hara?"

He grinned, and she couldn't help but laugh. "I grew up down here, remember?"

He came out of the bathroom with a towel wrapped around his hips and a dab of shaving cream still on his chin. He put his arms around her waist and pulled her against him. "We all grow up a little bit everywhere we go. Didn't you know that?"

"I suppose so."

"Are you going to take a shower?"

She leaned her head against him, trying to look up. "Want me to?"

"I'll ravish you with or without," he promised solemnly.

"I'm supposed to be resting, remember?"

"Vaguely."

She spun from his arms and headed for the shower. When she stepped under the water, she trembled slightly and wished that she weren't quite so eager for his touch. The warmth that had flashed through her when he had introduced her as his wife had been painful. She had so badly wanted it to be true.

She wanted this to last forever. Exploring old houses, walking together, feeling the sea breeze... wanting him.

She turned off the water and threw open the curtain. Ryan was there, grinning, his towel still around his waist.

"Did I ever tell you that you look great in water droplets?"

"You wear a towel very well yourself."

"Almost as well as I wear a sheet," he replied modestly. Then he reached for her, sweeping her off her feet and into his arms. Before she knew it she was lying on the soft bed, and his kisses were searing her naked flesh.

"Did I ever tell you," he whispered against the valley of her breasts, "that you taste just great in water droplets, too?"

"Never!" She laughed, but her laughter quickly faded as his hands moved over her, stroking her flesh. The searing moisture of his tongue followed the various intimate invasions of his touch with no hesitation and no mercy, and in a matter of moments she was on fire, wanting him. There was no laughter in his eyes when he rose over her, only the stark hunger of passion. It remained with him as he lowered himself slowly, penetrating her, filling her with the very life and soul of him.

Crying his name, she arched against him in a frenzy, and heat exploded all around her. She wound her arms around him, seeking all of him, feeling their flesh brush together, sleek and damp. She felt the strength of his arms and the hunger of his purpose, and always the strong thrust of his body, harder and harder, as if he would join them together for all time. The sweet sizzling excitement inside her rose ever higher, and still he urged her on. He whispered things she barely understood, yet knew innately. Then, when she could bear it no longer, he strained against her, his head thrown back, and a deep guttural cry escaped him. She barely heard herself echo his passion. She was aware of nothing but the ecstasy that held her, trembling, in its grasp.

After a little while she closed her eyes and slept. When she opened them again, he was watching her.

"I love you," he said quietly.

"What?" she whispered.

"I love you," he repeated. "I think I loved you from the moment I first saw you." He leaned over and kissed her mouth lightly, then pressed his lips to her throat. Finally he moved with leisurely abandon to the peak of her breast, and a sharp shudder of pleasure ran through her.

She plowed her fingers into his hair and drew his mouth to hers again. Then she moved away, just a fraction of an inch. "I . . . I love you, too."

He wrapped his arms around her and rolled her to her side. His hands skimmed down her back and then her buttocks, and he held her intimately, but tenderly and very tightly. His fingers continued to move.

"I love you . . ." she whispered again, amazed that she had dared to say the words out loud.

But then she remembered—quite vividly—the kiss he had received from the pretty red-haired nurse, and how intimately the two of them had been talking at the house. She stiffened in his arms.

"Oh, no!" he groaned against her flesh. He looked up to meet her eyes. "What?"

"The redhead," she said sweetly.

"What about her?"

"Well, you didn't just meet her. You admitted it. So just how well do you know her?"

"Well enough that she's promised to console me if you walk out on me again," Ryan said dryly.

"Did she console you the last time?"

He was silent, watching her. She wondered what he was thinking. One thing about Ryan was that as long as she had known him, he had never lied to her. But he took so long to reply that she felt a fierce shivering seize hold of her. "Ryan?"

"No," he said at last, flatly.

"Ryan—"

"Lucia, I never went out with her. She's a friend." He smiled ruefully. "Didn't you hear me? Or don't you understand? I love you. And I think you said—"

"I said that I love you, too," she whispered softly, gazing into his eyes.

"Then let's keep it at that for tonight. For once, Lucia, let's hold tight to the magic and keep it with us."

"Is it enough?" she whispered, afraid.

"It's incredible," he replied. "Hold me. Hold me again. Love me. Let's drown in it, and hold tight to the beauty of the moment."

She didn't need much convincing. She loved the taste of his mouth, and she felt as if she could kiss him forever. She loved the breadth of his shoulders and the broad expanse of his back and the tight muscles of his buttocks. She could hold him and touch him and explore his flesh forever.

And she could die a thousand times over when he touched her. When he kissed her, when he seared her flesh with his tongue, and when their limbs entangled and they met as one, breathless, wound together as if for eternity, straining to reach the stars. When it was over, she felt lethargic, but not too lethargic to revel in the sight of him.

"I love your toes," she told him after a while.

"I love yours."

"I'll bet you don't even know what they look like," she accused him.

"Well, I will admit that there are other parts of your anatomy that I can describe in greater detail. But your toes are charming. They're small, and you're wearing red nail polish."

"You're looking right at them."

"Aha. But you're looking right at mine, too."

She laughed, and somehow they wound up in one another's arms again. Then she swore that she was starving, so he released her, and they both showered quickly, packed up their things and headed for the restaurant.

The food was delicious, and the night was beautiful. Because of the way the room was arranged, it felt as if they were all alone, with a fine white wine and oysters on the half shell and wonderful fresh baked snapper. They might have been on their first date. She slipped off her shoe and ran her toes over his ankle, and he held her hand across the table.

There was a band playing, and they swayed slowly in one another's arms on the dance floor, not even bothering to speak.

Finally, at eleven, Lucia sighed softly. "We should drive back."

"We could just stay here," he said.

She shook her head. "I can't do that, and you know it."

"Your aunts and uncles are all in bed. They would never miss you."

"They might. And if they did, they would worry themselves sick. I just can't, Ryan. I thought you understood."

"I do," he said regretfully. "Okay, we'll go."

In the car, she leaned her head against his shoulder. Her window was down, and the night wind was cool and soft. It caressed her, just as the material of his jacket caressed her cheek, and the masculine scent of his after-shave stroked her senses. She wanted the drive to go on forever.

"Move back in with me?" he murmured softly.

She swallowed, trying not to stiffen against him. Earlier he had said that he loved her. Didn't that count for something?

Maybe not for enough. She was playing for all or nothing. She wanted him for all her life this time. She couldn't take another separation.

"I don't know."

"I do love you, Lucia."

"It just may not be...enough," she finished lamely.

He was silent, and she smiled painfully to herself. She knew him so well. She couldn't see his face, but she could imagine the flesh tightening over his cheeks as he clenched his jaw.

"Do you want me to come to Atlanta?" he finally asked.

"It isn't that...."

"Then what?"

"I—I need some time, Ryan."

He made a snorting sound. "How much time do you think we've got, Lucia? This vacation isn't going to go on forever."

"We have a week left."

"All right. A week. And when it ends, I want your answer. And if you leave me again, Lucia, so help me God, I hope you leave the country, because I don't want to go through this again. Ever!"

She leaned away from him, staring into the night, stunned by the depth of the hostility in his voice.

"Ryan—"

"No, Lucia, you wanted this week, so we won't say anything else until it's over. Then you make your decision."

"Ryan?"

"What!"

"I—I do love you."

Again he was silent. Then a sigh seemed to explode from him, and he reached out, cupping her neck, massaging it, his eyes still on the road. He drew her down until she was nestled on his lap. She looked up at him, and patterns of lights played over her face.

"Ryan?"

"What?"

"I loved you before, you know."

His eyes met hers for a moment; then he looked at the road. "You had a peculiar way of showing it," he said.

She opened her mouth to protest, then closed it again. Maybe, for the moment, what she had was enough.

She closed her eyes and curled against him, and a small smile played across her lips.

Ryan said nothing more, and the white Mercedes moved like a graceful cat through the night. Lucia fell asleep, and she didn't wake again during the two and a half hours it took to return to the condominium.

Ryan nudged her awake when they arrived. She blinked, smoothed her hair back and sat up. He laughed, watching her disorientation, then kissed her lightly on the lips.

"Want me to carry you up?" he asked her.

"No! I'm awake."

"Okay. Someone might be around, right?"

She cast him a withering glare. He laughed again, stepped out of the car, slammed his door and came around to open hers. She stumbled, and he held her up and led her toward the elevator.

"Too much wine," he said.

"I'm merely exhausted," she said.

"I'm not," he murmured regretfully, pushing the button for the elevator. She felt the way he was looking at her, met his eyes and flushed.

"Wouldn't it be nice if you were still living with me?" he whispered. "We could just come home together...."

She pulled away from him, smiling supremely. "No, I'm afraid not. Not with my family here."

"Isn't that rather hypocritical?"

"No, it's respectful!" she said, sweeping by him. She watched him punch the button for the penthouse. "Ryan!"

"Lucia, you're sleeping there tonight. I'm not. Remember? Dina has had a key all day."

"I forgot," Lucia admitted. "I forgot all about everything. About Lopez..."

"Then the day was worthwhile," Ryan said flatly. The elevator came to a halt, and he led her to the door. It was almost two o'clock, but there were still lights on in the penthouse. Lucia raised her hand to knock, but Ryan caught it and backed her against the door. And then he kissed her. He curved his hand over her breast and caressed it with erotic purpose, watching her eyes.

"Don't you wish, just a little bit, that we could be together all through the night?"

Lucia couldn't resist temptation. She yawned. He arched a brow, and she started to laugh softly, but then he moved his fingers in a softly caressing motion, and she leaned against him. "Yes, I do." She pushed him away. "But we can't. Good night, Mr. Dandridge."

"Good night, Ms. Lorenzo."

He stepped away, his hands folded behind his back. "Go on in."

She knocked. Dina answered the door in a long cranberry satin robe, but she seemed a little pale, and for once she didn't step past Lucia to say hello to Ryan.

Lucia said good-night to him again, then walked inside. She could hear his footsteps as he walked toward the elevator.

Dina closed and locked the door behind Lucia.

"What is it?" Lucia demanded.

"Someone went through our rooms today."

"What?"

"A man with a black briefcase. He was dressed in black, too. He opened our door with a key and he went through our rooms."

"Are you sure?"

"Yes."

"Did you—did you do anything?"

She shook her head. "I—I think Ryan sent him."

"What?"

"Well, he had a key."

Dina walked toward the kitchen, where what looked like a Bloody Mary was sitting on the counter. She took a long drink of it.

"Want a drink?" Dina said distractedly as she walked back and curled up on the couch, her feet tucked beneath her. Lucia followed, watching her.

"No! I want you to tell me what you're talking about."

"All right. I went back to sleep this morning. When I woke up, I came out on the terrace, just looking around. I thought Mom or one of the aunts might be around. I saw this man come to our floor, and he was acting very sneaky. Looking all around. Then I saw Hugh Buhler—"

"Who is Hugh Buhler?"

"The bug man."

"The bug man?"

"The exterminator!" Dina said impatiently.

"How do you know?"

Dina sighed with exasperation, pleating her robe with her free hand. "Because my mother meets everyone and instantly learns his—or her—life story within a matter of minutes. Ryan has a service—they come once a week. Anyway, once Hugh showed up, the man in the dark clothes hid!"

"What?"

"He hid. He ran back to the stairway and he hid. And he waited for Hugh to leave. Then he went back to our apartment, and he opened the door with a key!"

"So what makes you think Ryan knew about it? And why didn't you tell him just now?"

Dina flushed. "I should have called the police, I suppose. But I went downstairs, and the door was slightly ajar. I don't know what the guy was doing, but when I got near the door, I could hear him on the phone. And he was telling someone that he had checked it all out for Dandridge, and that he couldn't find a thing."

"What could he have been looking for?"

"Lopez?"

"He knew that Lopez wasn't in there!"

"Lucia, I don't know what's going on, and I'm scared!"

Lucia sat on the couch and stared straight ahead. "Ryan can't be guilty of anything," she murmured.

"What if he took you to Charleston all day just to get you out of the apartment?"

"It's his apartment—he could just have moved us if he'd wanted."

"Not if he didn't want to look suspicious."

"Ryan can't be guilty," Lucia said firmly, "because there's no way he could have moved that corpse the other night! I ran straight up to him!"

"But what if the corpse wasn't really there?"

"Dina, I saw it!"

"Maybe you did see Lopez on the beach. But maybe you were so scared and keyed up that you just imagined that you saw him the second time."

"No. I don't know what's going on, but Ryan can't be responsible."

"Lucia, if it isn't Ryan, it just might be someone we love, someone in the family!"

"I don't believe that, either."

"Then what?"

"I don't know. I don't know!"

"What are we going to do?"

"I don't know that, either!" Lucia moaned. She sat in silence for a moment, then rose. "Yes, I do."

"What?"

"I'm going to bed."

"To bed?"

"Yes, I'm exhausted. And if I get some sleep, things may start to make sense. Are you coming?"

"Yes! Let's double bolt everything and get in there together."

A few minutes later they were both stretched out on Ryan's king-size bed. Lucia heard Dina sigh softly.

"Lucia?"

"What?"

"If he turns out not to be a murderer, I really think you should marry that boy."

Lucia sat up. "What?"

"I said, if he turns out not to be a murderer—"

"He isn't a murderer!"

"Good. Then take some advice from me. Catch him and hold on tight."

"I'll keep it in mind," Lucia promised. She smoothed her hands over the sheets and closed her eyes, and she couldn't help but remember the night when they had lain in this bed together. She couldn't forget his touch, or his words.

Didn't she wish that they could go home together, lie down together, go to sleep together? he had asked.

But today had asked her to live with him again. Not to marry him, to live with him. And someone had gone into her room today—at his command. Maybe he had taken her to Charleston on purpose.

No. She wound her fingers into the sheets and held tight. He had said that he loved her today.

And for tonight, she wouldn't doubt him. Tonight she would make the love be enough, if only in her dreams.

Chapter 10

As tired as Lucia was, she didn't sleep late in the morning. She woke just before six, told herself she was insane and burrowed back under the covers. But there were too many things on her mind, and she couldn't get back to sleep. After ten minutes of staring at the wall, she gave up.

She hadn't brought any of her own things upstairs, but she discovered that Dina had taken care of the situation. She found her toothbrush in the bathroom, and one of her bathing suits, a red bikini, folded on the counter. She knew that it was early, but decided that a walk on the beach might be nice. Maybe when she got back Uncle Mario would be making some of his famous onion-studded hash brown potatoes. That would be nice.

She dressed in the bathing suit and checked on Dina, who was sleeping soundly.

Lucia left her a note, absconded with her beach robe and left Ryan's penthouse. She paused on the terrace. It was going to be a beautiful day. There was a gentle breeze, and the sky was etched with colors, gold and pink and crimson. The smell of the sea was in the air, and everything was perfect.

Lucia decided to run down the stairs instead of taking the elevator. The exercise felt good, but she was panting when she reached the bottom step. She saw her Uncle Mario. He and her cousin Joe were already stretched out on lawn chairs, reading the newspaper, a tin pot of espresso between them.

"Good morning!" Lucia called.

"Hey, *paisano*, good morning!" Uncle Mario walked over and kissed her. "We haven't seen much of you. Where have you been? Off falling in love, huh? Want some espresso?"

"I'd love some espresso." She was awfully glad of the second question.

"Mind taking Joey's cup?"

She glanced at Joe. He was blinking against the sun and watching her peculiarly.

"I don't mind at all."

Joe grinned at her. "Lots of sugar, Dad. Lucia hates it without sugar."

"Sugar, lots of it," Uncle Mario said. He fixed Lucia a demitasse of the strong coffee and pulled up a chair for her. "Where have you been, sweetie?"

"I went into Charleston yesterday, with Ryan Dandridge."

"You did? Well, good for you. Did you have a good time?"

"Yes, thanks."

"You coming with us to dinner tonight?"

"All of us in one restaurant? Of course. I wouldn't miss it for the world."

Joe was still watching her. "You inviting Ryan?"

She stared at him. "Should I?"

"Yeah, I think you should."

"And if I don't invite him, you will?"

"Am I missing something here?" Uncle Mario asked.

Lucia shook her head. "No, no." She sipped the espresso. It was delicious. Her uncle could make great hash browns and wonderful espresso. It was a good thing she lived in Atlanta, she decided. Though her own mother was a fabulous cook, Lucia had learned to say no when Patience was pushing extra helpings. But it was impossible to say no to her aunts and uncles.

"That Ryan, he's a nice boy."

"Yes, he is."

"He's not Italian, but he's a nice boy."

Lucia lowered her head, trying not to smile. "Yes, Uncle Mario."

"You like him?"

"Uncle Mario!"

"Dad," Joe interceded. "I could really go for some more espresso. And I'll bet Bill will be down soon. You know he loves this stuff."

"You think so? Well, I'll go make another pot. With my luck that Gino Lopez will come by for some. Though come to think of it, I've seen even less of him than I have of Lucia for the last few days."

Lucia froze, watching her uncle. He had spoken ruefully, bluntly. He had to be innocent. What should she do? Should she tell him that Gino Lopez would never be by again to drink his espresso? She could just imagine herself saying casually, *"Oh, Uncle Mario, don't worry. Gino Lopez is dead. I can't prove it, because I can't find his body right now, but I saw it once on the beach, and then again in my bathtub."*

"Your bathtub, you say?"

"Yes, my bathtub. But then he disappeared from there too...."

Uncle Mario started for the elevator, and Joe interrupted her reverie by asking, "So how's life, little cousin?"

She cast him a slow, careful look. "I don't know, Joe. You tell me. What's going on with you?"

"With me. Nothing."

"Why do you always look like the cat who ate the canary?"

"I do not."

"You do."

Joe shrugged. "Well, I have this friend, you see...."

"Go on," Lucia said.

Joe was grinning away. He didn't seem to be able to help himself. "I wish I could have been there."

"Where?"

"In your room. The morning when you and Ryan collided on the bed."

Lucia gasped, stunned. "Joe! You set that up on purpose!"

"I was afraid you might not talk to each other if I didn't set something up."

"Damn it, Joe! Then Ryan *did* know—"

"No, Lucia, Ryan is innocent of whatever you're about to accuse him of. I just put two and two together. I knew that you spent the winter in Rhode Island without seeing any of us—which was very strange. And I knew that Ryan was there. And then he suddenly returned in an awful temper, and he didn't go out on dates anymore, and I knew something had happened. A little checking up assured me that the object of his *amore* was my own dear sweet cousin, Lucia Lorenzo.''

She stared at him openmouthed. He tapped her chin, closing her jaw for her. Lucia hesitated for a moment, faltering. "Joe, you had no right. You had no right at all."

"Lucia, don't be such a stubborn little coward."

"I am not a coward."

"You are. You want something, so go and get it!"

"Joe, you don't understand. It isn't me. It's your friend. Oh, never mind. Why am I trying to talk to you?" She groaned.

"You should be talking to Ryan."

Lucia rose, smiling at him sweetly. "I'm going to the beach. See you later."

His laughter followed her as she leaped over the wall to the beach. She walked down to the water and kicked at the surf. It was going to be a hot day. She stared up at the sun, and it was nearly blinding. She blinked quickly, turned around to face the condo again and opened her eyes.

A gasp escaped her.

Gino Lopez was on one of the balconies. Or at least his *body* was. He was leaning over the railing, and he was still wearing his swimming trunks.

Then the sun rose higher, shooting painful rays into her eyes, and she blinked again.

In that short time, the body disappeared.

"No!" she cried. She started running toward the condo, then paused. She didn't know which balcony it had been! She had been blinking from the sun, and then she had been so startled that she hadn't really paid attention to which balcony held the body!

"Damn!" she swore in frustration. But it was there—somewhere.

She leaped over the wall again and hurried across the pool area. Joe stared at her, his sunglasses in place, the newspaper in his hands.

Well, Joe was innocent, she decided. But Uncle Mario...

Uncle Mario had just returned to his room—to make more coffee. Or so he had said. And the rest of the family were all still in their apartments. Not even the children were out yet.

"Lucia!" Joe called.

She ignored him and pressed the button for the elevator. When it didn't come, she raced to the stairs.

On the second floor, she paused. Uncle Mario and Aunt Faith were just stepping out of their apartment. "Good morning, Lucia!" Aunt Faith called to her. "You *are* coming to dinner tonight, right?"

"Uh—right!" Lucia responded.

Then they were all startled by an explosion of angry words coming from Lucia's and Dina's apartment. Aunt Faith looked quickly from her husband to Lucia. "That's Ron Lopez's voice!" she said.

Lucia realized that her aunt was right. Then she heard Ryan's voice, quiet and deadly, before Ron Lopez's voice flared out again.

"Is Dina in there?" Uncle Mario demanded. He looked as if he was about to barge through the door.

Lucia shook her head. "Dina and I traded the penthouse for our condo last night. Dina is sleeping upstairs, Uncle Mario."

"You did it, Dandridge!" Ron Lopez's voice suddenly came to them very clearly. "Because you owed him—"

"No. I paid my debts years ago."

The voices fell again. Lucia felt acutely uncomfortable, standing there listening to it all, with her aunt and uncle.

She had to get away. She didn't want to find the body anymore. She just wanted to get away. She had to go somewhere.

"Excuse me!" she said, flashing her aunt and uncle a quick smile before she turned and fled. She hurried back to the beach, where she started walking.

She didn't stop until she was far away, and then she sat down in the sand, hugged her knees and felt the sun on her shoulders as she leaned her face into her hands. She was in love with Ryan. And she was afraid that he was a murderer.

How could she love him and suspect him of such a thing? If she loved him, she should defend him. He couldn't have killed Lopez!

But if he hadn't done it...then maybe one of her uncles had.

She didn't know what to think, what to feel. She was in love with Ryan, and he had said that he loved her, even if he hadn't managed yet to come around to proposing marriage. His love was something special. But she was so afraid....

She lay down in the sun and felt its warmth wash over her. She felt numb inside, and she closed her eyes and just lay there.

Sometime after noon she headed back. She wanted to see Ryan desperately, yet she was afraid to see him.

He was nowhere around. Instead, Lucia found Dina and Theresa and Sophie with the kids on the beach. "The guys are out golfing," Theresa told Lucia.

"That's nice."

"Ryan is with them," Sophie offered.

"That's nice."

"So how's your love life?" Theresa demanded.

"Better than mine!" Dina sighed, but she offered Lucia a wavering smile.

Even Dina was afraid of Ryan, Lucia thought.

"Joe said to tell you that he invited Ryan to dinner tonight," Theresa told Lucia. "He was afraid you might have forgotten."

"How thoughtful of him," Lucia murmured.

"I think you should tell all," Sophie said solemnly.

Lucia started. Tell all? What were they talking about?

"Charleston!" Theresa said. "How was your day in Charleston?"

"Oh, it was, umm, fine. We had a really good time. Hey, want me to take Tracy in the water for a while?"

"Sure, thanks," Theresa said.

Lucia took Tracy in her arms. It felt good to hold her little cousin, and it was nice to see her beautiful, innocent smile.

"Hey, you're not getting out of anything!" Sophie called to Lucia as she headed for the water. "We want all the details in living color!"

"Dream on!" Lucia called back.

She played in the water with Tracy for a while, then walked back up the beach and announced that she was going to go in and take a nap before dinner. Dina was ready to go in with her. "We're back in our own apartment," she said. "It was just too hard to start moving everything."

Lucia thought about telling Dina that she had seen the body again, then decided against it. She was starting to think she was losing her mind herself.

A little while later, the phone rang. It was Sophie. There was going to be a cocktail hour at five in her apartment, then the younger generation was going to play an hour of goony golf before meeting the aunts and uncles at seven-thirty for dinner.

By five they were outside Sophie's condo. Leon opened the door and whistled at both of them. Lucia saw that Ryan was already there. He had a fawn jacket thrown over his shoulders, and he was in stone-washed jeans and a navy polo shirt. He was standing by the sofa, sipping a beer with Joe. His eyes fell on her, and he smiled, but she wasn't sure the smile touched his eyes.

"Aunt Faith made stuffed mushrooms. Help yourself," Sophie said, offering a tray to Lucia.

Leon brought her a glass of white wine. "I like that outfit. It's a pity we're related, because you are awfully cute," he told Lucia.

She was wearing a white halter dress with a wide red belt, red beads and earrings, and sandals. It was a good outfit for her, she knew. The white emphasized her tan, and the red was good against the darkness of her hair and eyes. Ryan's eyes were on her again, and she thought that he appreciated the outfit, too. But then he looked away, as if he hadn't really been paying attention to her after all.

Why should he? He had other things on his mind. He'd started the morning off with a big argument with the son of a man he might have killed....

They didn't linger in the apartment long before heading for goony golf. They had the older children with them, while the aunts and uncles had the babies. From the way that Ryan moved purposefully toward Lucia, she knew she would be riding with him. "Hey, Theresa, Ryan and I will take the twins, okay?" she asked.

"Sure!" Theresa called back.

If Ryan was puzzled by her action, he didn't show it. In the parking lot Lucia quickly ushered the boys into the back seat, then chatted nonstop with them while Ryan drove. She caught his eyes once. Now he *was* puzzled.

The women played against the men once they got to the golf course. Theresa and Sophie each made a hole in one right off the bat. The men—the real golfers in the group—took several strokes.

"We're just trying to make you feel good," Leon said.

"Sure. Women like to feel superior," Bill added, nodding sagely.

"Right," his wife said, stepping by him to the next hole. She tugged on his earlobe. "It's because we *are* superior," she said sweetly.

"Hey, we're not going to take that!" Joe protested.

"Sure we are," Bill said, his eyes sparkling as he pulled Theresa into his arms. "I want her coming home in a good mood."

Everyone laughed except Lucia, who felt Ryan watching her. He caught up to her, alone, when they got to the third hole. "What the hell is the matter with you?" he demanded.

"Nothing!"

"Nothing?"

"All right, Ryan. I saw the body again today."

"What? When? Where?"

"On the balcony. Your balcony, I think. My balcony, I mean. The balcony where you were staying this morning!"

"Lucia, you're nuts!"

"I'm not! And I also..."

"You also what?"

"I also heard you arguing with Ron Lopez. Aunt Faith and Uncle Mario heard you, too, so don't deny it!"

"So what?"

"He accused you of murdering his father."

Ryan stepped back. "Oh. So that makes me guilty."

"I didn't say that."

"I hope my life is never at stake with you on the jury."

"Ryan—"

He didn't wait to hear what she had to say. He rejoined the men and didn't speak to her for the rest of the game.

Despite her less-than-adequate playing, the women easily triumphed over the men, and everyone—or nearly everyone—left in good spirits. Lucia talked to the twins again as they drove to the restaurant, and Ryan didn't even glance her way.

The restaurant was wonderful. Their table was on an open terrace facing the beach. There were candles stuck in wine bottles, and the tablecloths were all red and white checked cotton. The lights were muted, and the music was as soft as the sea breeze.

Everyone was talking and joking and laughing, having a thoroughly good time. But Lucia couldn't bring herself to look at Ryan sitting beside her. It was achingly good to be with him, to see him with her family, to see him laugh and fit in. And yet it was also very painful, because she didn't know what was going on, and she certainly didn't know what to do.

In between the appetizers and the main course, she suddenly couldn't stand it anymore. All she wanted was to have Ryan's arm casually around her shoulders, the way Bill's arm fell around Theresa. She wanted the laughter; she wanted the warmth. She wanted the trust, but no matter how close she came to it, it seemed to elude her.

"Excuse me, I'll be right back," she said suddenly, standing up.

"Hey, wait, I'll come with you," Theresa began.

"See that!" Bill complained. "Women! They just can't go to the bathroom alone. It's pathetic, isn't it?"

"Pathetic," Joe agreed.

"All right, I won't go now!" Theresa said with a dramatic sigh.

"No, no—"

"Hey, I'll be right back!" Lucia said again. She wasn't going to the bathroom. She just wanted to be alone for a minute.

Ryan's eyes caught hers.

He knows, she thought, but she turned around anyway. She walked along the terrace as if she were heading for the ladies' room, but then she made a sharp turn and started for the beach.

The night was as beautiful as the day had been. The stars were out, a shower of diamond shards against black velvet. The rush of the surf was soft and compelling, and the moon was covered by a slight haze.

They had to talk, really talk, she thought. She had to be honest with him, and she had to pray that he would be honest with her. They had to find out the truth about Lopez. And then they had to find out the truth about themselves.

There was a sudden noise behind her. She started to turn, unalarmed, certain that Ryan had followed her.

Something cracked against her head. The pain was searing, and a new array of stars burst before her eyes. She fell to the ground, dazed, unable to see anything. Hands gripped her ankles and started to pull her.

"Lucia!"

She heard Joe's voice, and suddenly she was released. Time passed. She fought the dizziness; she tried to call to Joe.

"Lucia!" This time it was Ryan calling her, and she struggled to sit up. The pain began to ease, and she touched the back of her head, where she discovered a huge lump.

"Lucia! Lucia!"

She stumbled to her feet. The ocean waved before her, and then her vision started to clear. Ryan was almost on top of her, and Joe was right behind him.

There was no one on the beach besides the two of them. No one at all. Just Joe and Ryan, two of the men she loved most in the world.

One of them had struck her, doubled back, then pretended to come back again, searching for her.

She was losing her mind. She was absolutely losing her mind. She was also very frightened.

"Lucia!" Ryan stood before her and caught her hands. "Lucia, why didn't you answer me? You scared everyone, disappearing like that."

"I, er, I—"

"Lucia!" Joe snapped, panting as he reached her. "I called and called. Boy, when Ryan lit out after you and then didn't return, we all panicked."

"I tripped. That's all."

"You tripped?" Ryan said suspiciously.

"Yes. In the sand." She forced herself to smile, even though her head was killing her. She wanted to get back to the condominium, lock herself in her room and call Sergeant Mahoney. She didn't care anymore if he thought she was crazy. She wanted to tell him everything. And she couldn't bear sitting beside Ryan any longer, feeling the heat of his thigh next to hers, the burning questions in his eyes....

She had to be careful, though. "I'm sorry I frightened you," she said sweetly. "Let's get back to the restaurant, okay?"

She started off across the sand. The two men held back, staring after her in astonishment before they finally followed her.

She sat down and sipped some wine, picked at both her eggplant and calamari, then excused herself again. She stopped at Aunt Faith's table and whispered to her aunt that she wasn't feeling well, so she was going to grab a cab and go home.

It was a mistake. She should have known not to say a word about her health.

"Lucia! Poor darling! You are not calling any cab. Uncle Mario will take you home."

"No, I'll take you home," Uncle Paul said, rising.

By then Ryan had heard the commotion, and he was rising, too. "Lucia, what's wrong? You know I'll take you."

She latched on to Uncle Paul's arm, since he was already standing. "No! Don't you dare leave, Ryan. You'll stay if you take me home, and Uncle Paul will come right back." She offered Ryan a dazzling smile. "I think I just need a little bit of sleep. I'll see you later, all right?"

"No, Lucia, I brought you—"

"Son, it's all right. You stay," Uncle Paul insisted.

Lucia saw a pulse ticking at Ryan's throat, but without being totally rude to her uncle, he had little choice but to acquiesce. He caught Lucia's hand. "I'll check on you later, okay?"

She nodded. "Yes, thanks, Ryan."

As Uncle Paul led her from the restaurant, she knew Ryan was still watching her.

Uncle Paul chatted as they drove. They talked about the vacation, and how nice it was to all be together. "I think we should do it every year."

"It's wonderful," Lucia agreed.

"The kids love the beach. So do us old folks. And then there's cocktail hour for your generation and antacids for mine."

Lucia laughed and patted his leg. "You'll never be old, Uncle Paul."

"Well, I'm not exactly a spring chicken, but I enjoy life. Remember that, Lucia. Enjoy life. And share it. Your aunt and I, we've shared good times and bad for over forty years now. That's the way to do it. And if I'm always young, it's because I'm young in her eyes." He swung into the parking lot. "You look for that, Lucia. Love. It's the only really important thing in life."

Lucia kissed his cheek. "I'll keep it in mind, Uncle Paul."

"I'll walk you up to your room."

Lucia stepped out of the car and turned to him firmly. "You will not! You'll drive back to that restaurant."

"I'll walk you up."

She wasn't going to convince him, so she slipped her key from her bag, and Uncle Paul took it from her and opened the door. He stepped into the hallway and looked around.

For a moment a sizzle of fear shot through Lucia. Uncle Paul hated Lopez. Uncle Paul had done the deed, and now he had brought her back here, alone, in the dark...

He handed her the key. "Get some sleep, princess," he said. Then he left, closing the door behind him.

A minute later Lucia began to laugh. She hated herself, but she began to laugh. She was going mad, suspecting her uncle, who had always loved her dearly and treated her generously.

Suddenly she heard something, and the hair rose on her nape and goose bumps formed all along her arms. Someone was in her bathroom. No, in her room, going through her drawers.

Lucia started along the hall, hugging the wall. When she reached the door to her darkened room, she glanced in and saw a man carrying a flashlight.

It wasn't Ryan. That much she knew. Her heart began to thump.

The man swung around suddenly, and the flashlight beam hit her in the face. "I know you're there, Ms. Lorenzo."

Lopez! *Ron* Lopez!

She didn't know what he had done, or what he wanted. She only knew that he was dangerous. She screamed and plunged past the open doorway, flung open the door to the condo and tore toward the elevator. She slammed her hand against the button, but nothing happened, and she swerved, racing for the stairway.

She heard a strange, whizzing sound, and something crashed into the wood of the stairway. A bullet, she thought, amazed. He was shooting at her!

She ran down the stairs, screaming. She could hear his footsteps as he pounded after her, and she screamed again and again, but she knew it would be to no avail. She was alone. Everyone was at the restaurant.

She headed for her car, but it was locked, and she didn't have her keys.

Ryan's car was there! But where the hell was Ryan?

She couldn't go back. She couldn't even run for the street. Ron Lopez was back there, chasing her and carrying a gun.

There was only one way to go—toward the beach.

She veered around the pool, gasping for breath. Suddenly a pair of arms shot out and grabbed her, and she screamed, loudly and desperately.

"Lucia!" It was Ryan. She met his steady gaze, her own eyes glazed and terrified. "Lucia, what in God's name—"

Another bullet whizzed by in the darkness. "What the hell?" Ryan demanded.

"It's Lopez! Ron Lopez!"

"We can't go toward the street," Ryan said, shoving her toward the beach. "Run!"

He was right behind her. He practically threw her over the wall, then jumped down beside her. The sand was already soaked. The tide was coming in, and Lucia realized that she would never get anywhere in her high-heeled sandals, so she ripped them off and threw them away. Ryan caught her hand, and they started running again, sloshing through the dark water.

They heard a curious muffled sound as a bullet cut through the water and was buried in the sand. Gasping, Lucia looked at Ryan. "Can't you do something?"

"I haven't got a gun on me, sorry."

"Oh, Ryan! You could get shot—for me!"

"I should have a gun on me," he admitted, apologizing. "I knew something was going on."

"Stop!" Lopez called from behind. "Come on, we'll talk about this."

"Keep going. His stamina is failing," Ryan ordered her.

"*His* stamina?" Lucia whispered.

Her legs hurt, her lungs were on fire, and the soles of her feet felt as if they were in ribbons. The lights from the hotels lent a glow to the beach, but the tide was up, almost covering the sand, and the water brought its own brand of darkness.

Suddenly she tripped on something beneath the surface and screamed, almost going down. Ryan pulled her up and threw her over his shoulder. "You'll never make it with me!" she whispered to him, trying to right herself as she dangled over his back.

"If I don't make it *with* you, I don't care if I make it *without* you," Ryan said.

"Ryan, that was beautiful."

"Thank you." Another bullet flew by. "Damn it! Shut up and let me run, will you? I really would like to have a future with you—if we live that long. A married future."

"A *married* future? Ryan, would you actually marry me?"

"Would *you* actually marry *me*?"

"I asked first."

"Lucia, I wanted to marry you when you ran away from me."

"I was afraid that you'd never marry me!"

"You went through that annulment...."

"I just needed to know that this time it would be forever. Oh, Ryan, I do want it all! I want marriage and children and a big church wedding with dozens of flowers—"

She broke off as they heard the loud splashing of water behind them. Ryan moved so suddenly that her chin slammed against his back. "We're both going to die single if we don't do something quick." Ryan said. He was running again, running hard, for their lives.

"The dock!" he cried suddenly.

They had reached the fishing dock, and she could see other people there. Lopez wouldn't dare shoot them down in front of witnesses.

Ryan set her down on the wooden surface. "Can you walk?"

Lucia nodded, and he hopped up beside her. In the glow of the lights, they could see Lopez behind them. Ryan grabbed her hand and started to run.

"He won't follow us," Ryan said confidently.

Lucia looked back. "Ryan."

"What?"

"He *is* following us."

"Damn!"

He jerked her along at a greater pace. People turned and stared at them, and someone screamed at the sight of Lopez, racing after them, his gun held high. Another shot was fired and sank into the wood.

"That's six, at least!" Lucia cried.

Another shot rang out. "Lucia, you watch too many westerns!" Ryan said. "He could have two dozen shots in that thing!"

They had reached the seaward end of the dock. "Jump," Ryan said. Then, without giving her time to respond, he picked her up and tossed her over. She felt as if she were falling forever, then suddenly she hit the water. It was cold, and she sank quickly, the frigid darkness enveloping her. As she fought to return to the surface, fingers clutched her hair, grasping and pulling.

"Lucia!" Ryan cried in relief as she broke the surface.

"Ryan!"

He wrapped his arms around her and they treaded water together for a moment. Then he brought them over to the pilings and wrapped his arms around one, anchoring them. His eyes remained locked on hers as they heard footsteps above. Then Ron Lopez called out to them wildly.

"Dandridge! Where are you? Dandridge, so help me, I'll get you, I'll find you!"

"I love you," Ryan said to Lucia. "And I want to spend my life with you."

"You'll really marry me?"

"As soon as possible. This chaste act around your family is killing me. We are allowed to sleep together once we're legally wed, aren't we?"

She smiled. "Of course. But, Ryan, you said you weren't the type to fall in love forever and—"

"I wasn't. But then I fell in love with you, and I knew that it could be forever for us. But I was afraid. I'd never felt that way before. And you were so adamant about not marrying again."

"But I knew that I loved you, really loved you. And I ran away because I couldn't stand it if it wasn't going to be forever."

"We do have one problem."

"What's that?"

"Lopez is still up there."

But Lopez wasn't up there anymore. They heard a sudden, huge splash.

"Lopez!" Lucia shouted.

Ryan set her arms around the piling and swam toward the spot where Lopez had landed. In the darkness, Lucia could see nothing. "Ryan!" she screamed. A moment later two heads broke the surface. "Ryan!" she called again as the heads went back under.

She heard the thunder of footsteps above her, and a searchlight was suddenly trained on the ocean. A voice came over a loudspeaker. "This is the police. Show yourselves—"

Just then Ryan's head broke the surface of the water, and he waved against the spotlight. Lucia saw that he had Lopez by the nape of the neck. "Mahoney?"

"Dandridge?"

"Yeah. Get me some help down here, will you?"

"Help is coming."

A moment later an officer stripped off his shoes and dived into the water. Someone else lowered a rope, and the officer and Ryan looped it around an unconscious Lopez. Then Ryan returned to Lucia.

"Are you all right?"

She nodded, then grimaced. "Ryan?"

"What?"

"Something bit my toe, and I'm awfully glad I didn't see what it was."

Ryan laughed, then wrapped his arms around her and kissed her. All of a sudden he lost his grip, and they plummeted into the sea together. They came up gasping and laughing.

"We're about to drown each other," Lucia warned him.

"I'd gladly die for you."

Her eyes sparkled. "Not on your life. Not until you marry me."

Half an hour later they were seated on the dock. Lucia was wrapped in a blanket and holding a cup of coffee. Uncle Mario, Aunt Faith, Dina and Joe were there, and Ryan was trying to explain things to everyone while the police tried to piece together the story.

"He talked for a few minutes," Sergeant Mahoney said to Ryan. "Ron Lopez, that is. It seems he fought with his father and shoved him. When Gino fell, he struck his head on the fencing around the pool. No one saw it, and Ron panicked. He put the body down on the beach. He was desperate. He had to get rid of it. He hadn't meant to kill his father, but once Gino was dead, Ron decided to cash in on some of his father's, er, business deals. Then you started hounding him. He wanted you to be accused of murder. He was trying to set that up, but then you and Ms. Lorenzo suddenly appeared. He had to hide the body again, so he stashed it in her bathroom. No one would believe she was guilty of the crime, so when she discovered the body, he had to get rid of it again."

"I still don't understand!" Aunt Faith moaned. "Lucia, you say that Gino's body kept appearing—and you didn't even tell us!"

"Well, it kept disappearing, too, Aunt Faith," Lucia apologized.

"We didn't want to upset you, Mom," Dina explained.

"You knew!"

"Well, I knew what Lucia told me."

"I, er, I was afraid that—" Lucia began.

"Oh, no!" Aunt Faith wailed. "You thought that one of us—oh, Lucia! How could you?"

Uncle Mario began to laugh when Aunt Faith complained that she might be about to pass out.

"At least Ryan is innocent," Dina said.

"You suspected Ryan!" Joe protested indignantly.

Ryan was staring at Lucia. "I never really suspected you!" she said. "Well, except that you did have someone go through our room. And tonight, on the beach, I thought that you hit me on the head—"

"Someone hit you on the head?" Ryan and Joe thundered simultaneously.

"I, uh..."

"She thought it was one of us," Joe told Ryan indignantly.

"I didn't really...."

"Liar," Ryan said softly. He ran his hand over her damp hair, pulling her head tenderly against him. "I'm still going to marry you. But it may take a little while to forgive and forget."

"Marry!" Aunt Faith gasped. "But you barely know one another!"

"Wrong, Ma," Joe said. "They know each other very well."

"What?"

"We know each other very, *very* well," Ryan said softly, and he kissed Lucia tenderly, for everyone to see.

Aunt Faith sighed. "It's really okay, Joe?"

"It's really okay."

It was just fine with Lucia. Ryan was still kissing her. They probably both smelled like dead fish, and they were covered in seaweed and were soaking wet, but it didn't matter at all. He was all the warmth she would ever need.

"Oh! A wedding. A wedding in the family! A big, wonderful Italian wedding with music and food—"

"Maybe she just wants a quiet wedding, Mom," Dina suggested.

"And the tarantella!" Aunt Faith concluded.

Ryan stopped kissing Lucia for just one moment, and his eyes sparkled as they met hers. "I'm sure a tarantella will be just fine."

Lucia grinned. "A huge orchestra and a half dozen attendants?"

"Two dozen, if you want."

"Oh, Ryan."

"Oh, Lucia."

He kissed her again, and everyone on the dock applauded.